THE JOURNEY OF STYLES

Uluru The Floating Pebble

Damien Renwick

CONTENTS

TRANSLATOR'S SUMMARY

The Journey of Styles is one that could never be understood if it were not for the constant retellings of its story. The book was first discovered in the Barthes farmhouse near the town of St Cecile de Cayrou in South West France in the year of 2008. The handwritten book enclosed in a sealed envelope dated 1812. A brief note written in French gave the date and location of where the book had been discovered. Knights of St John Monastery, Valetta Malta. 1783 by French forces.

The original book was written Hebrew and chronicled the travels of an Australian man known as Styles. The events that took place in the years 1771 to 1783. The events that occur are strikingly similar to the events of Cook and others towards the end of the 1800's. However no such documented voyages occurred.

The story was told by an unknown narrator and the events within recounted the travels of a man from Australia known as Styles. Due to the long periods of time Styles spends alone in the book it can only be assumed that he is in fact the author. An argument against this would be that the narrator never once calls himself Styles. If the story was true we could assume it was told orally by Styles to an as yet unidentified scribe.

In modern times we find ourselves once again presented

with the truth. It is the year 2020 and with the internet, we find ourselves able to find any truth. It seems this book was written for the future generations - one in fact - this one. As we search for answers we find they were already found. They were waiting for us all along.

THE FLOATING PEBBLE

YEAR 39,993

Styles took a deep breath as if preparing for underwater submersion. Then he stopped drumming. He watched as one hundred thousand drums played on together. All the tribes of Astraliyah encircled Uluru, the sacred stone of all the people. A culmination of forty thousand years had resulted in this meeting.

The multitudes of people stood in rows around the giant pebble playing their music; sound blasting down the long side of the lozenge shaped pebble that was six miles around. While the low boom of the drum induced a natural state amongst the people, he surveyed the crowd for his father, PinPin, amongst the thousands. His vision was hazy. The air burned from song. As beautiful as it was, it had become extremely dangerous.

His father had left his post. His voice was needed to complete the raising. Realising his father was nowhere to be seen he decided to retreat a safe distance away from the pebble to a hill. As every one else played and hummed Styles stepped back through the rows of people in search of his father. The first man he stepped past was dressed as a can-garoo.

The sweat and fear on this man's face spoke volumes, far higher than the drums. He looked at Styles and continued banging on his instrument, singing along. With a blink, the man convinced Styles to turn around and forward look. As he did, he could hardly believe his eyes.

The giant pebble that represented the wholeness of all his people seemed to be growing taller, like a tree. Ignoring the scornful eyes of the man, worryingly, Styles took more steps back. Undeterred by the madness, he turned and began to run, running beyond the rows of drummers away from the pebble.

All the faces gazed at him and on he ran, finding his father was more important now. If his father did not return there would be unbearable repercussions. It was then that he saw his father, PinPin, running in the distance towards another man. It must have been a quarter of a mile beyond the last row of drummers.

'Where is he going?' he thought to himself.

Feeling weird, as he was the only person not playing an instrument, he ran towards to his father. On he pushed through the waves of human barriers who for the most part stared beyond him to the sky.

The last two people who stood like gates clocked him. Undeterred, he ran on before they could stop him. Able to focus on the face of the man that his father had risked the life of a hundred thousand people for, he saw the face of the human, dressed in clothes unlike any other. The man had skin the colour of cheese and with eyes squinting in the afternoon light. His hands held PinPin's drum, easy to recognise with its barrel of seven colours.

His father began waving his hands around and pointing, they were communicating. PinPin was not happy at all. The human backed away holding PinPin's drum and PinPin pointed backwards towards Styles. As he did, the man froze stiff dropping the instrument. PinPin shook his head and turned, leaving the man and walking towards a cave in the distance.

The human looked amazed. Styles turned to see what he was looking at. His jaw dropped just as the base of Uluru rose beyond the height of everyone's head and kept rising.

The air was filled with heat and the vibration of sound. The very electricity that flowed throughout the Afro's of 100,000 people. The intense mass of the bedrock was un-paralleled, unequalled, unrivalled.

One by one, rows of drums began to beat together, the wave culminating in a choir of humming. Nine hundred and ninety thousand, nine hundred and ninety eight Afros glowed purple. Styles froze. Unable to move, he just stared. Uluru was floating in the air to the sound of music. The world's largest pebble is just floating there. Now with it floating, the other half of a royal symphony could just be seen far away on what had been the other side of Uluru.

Someone yelled in elation. Others followed and soon the ground roared once more as innumerable arms tilted boomerangs up to the sky. Like a mass flock of electric eagles the boomerangs fibrillated themselves in the float-ing shadow of Uluru. The wood and silver hurricane took on a unified form of a rainbow snake, the great spirit of the people.

Atop Uluru the crowds screamed and applauded, watch-ing from the edges. Those on the ground yelled back in vic-tory over the dreamtime as all the boomerangs fell to the ground. Mankind was about to upgrade. Free falling to a halt, the drums receded, till only the wind could be heard. Then the noise of the bass dropped and one hundred thou-sand wind instruments rang out from the far side of where Uluru used to sit. Uluru had risen so high in to the sky that the sun was partially blocked from view. The people atop Uluru, unheard, begged for help.

PinPin was pre-destined to lead the royal symphony. The chosen 32 Flute Crew of the Peruvian School Of Music waited. Smiles crept on the faces of the people. The shadow of Uluru hovered over the crowds on the ground, which only Styles had noticed. Proudly they all began to descend in to the large sapphire city that until now had been hidden from view. The first people to enter the city were those waiting for Uluru to rise, entering from the south. Rays of light agitated the ground under Uluru. Sun-lit solar stores fired up and large purple crystals as big as trees beamed through a maze.

An enormous stone bath in the centre of the city re-flected in to the sky. The overall pattern – a kaleidoscope – projected on to the base of Uluru a vast contorted rainbow of indigo and purple hues, mightily resembling a winged serpent.

Many cried and chanted, "Hawah Uluru!" as the pebble floated effortlessly in the sky for all the people to see.

They danced towards the city on the ground, row by row entering their new home and for a moment all seemed well. Styles looked back for PinPin and the human. Yet again his attention returned to Uluru and the people.

Uluru began to move in dangerous ways, swaying this way and that. Styles' stomach began to make strange noises. Then he tensed up. He knew it was too late now, too late to help. He could only hope the giant pebble was a slave to the music and would obey the people. Still he knew it needed exactly everyone to play. Styles had not managed to get his father back among the people.

He backed away until he was at his father's drum, he tried carrying it but it was too heavy. He tried banging on it but his arms were not strong enough and his hands not skilled enough to hit the right note. Yet, he banged on it, with all his might.

People turned to look and soon people began talking, realising whose drum it was. Some people spread word that a member of the group was not where they were sup-posed to be. As he tried to be play along with all of his kin-folk he turned his head in the direction of PinPin. He could barely make him out.

The drumming seemed to make no difference from where he was standing. People screamed out as he dropped the drum and ran towards PinPin. He had made it on to a large hill when he stopped. Someone was screaming and in the moment – only for that moment - when the music went quiet a woman's voice cried out, "Styles".

He turned to see the inner circle had all descended the large city of stone that had previously been covered by Uluru. A woman now made it out of the last row of drummers. Then the music came back again in full swing. The woman was his mother, but it was too late. The floating colossus of a pebble that shadowed them began to dip - dipping thousands of people like a speck of dust and mud - thousands of his people.

Horror rang out and the music turned in to a symphony of tragedy. Most that fell from the edge fell straight away to the ground. There were some that slowed their descent and span and then there was one that hovered with some unseen force far from the spillage in the sky. For a mere 7 seconds the single body hovered above the Kalkatungan nation. Then surely as that single body saw their loved ones fall to certain ending, it decided it would join them. It fell like all the others.

That's when the music stopped. People ran back and forth as the giant pebble that is as large as a city, began its 600 metre free-fall. Like ants under the shadow of the pebble, thousands of people who had not yet entered the many entrances in to the ground scrambled about. Chaos ensued. Styles cringed as he turned his back on the impending event.

He started to run again and ran as fast as he could. He turned around to see the face his mother, tribe and friends, no doubt looking for PinPin and himself. Uluru's descent from the sky was almost complete. All the singing had gone from a synchronized choir to a mass of screaming and screeching voices. Not all the people would make it in to the interior of Uluru's protection.

The rock came down to a crashing halt, landing exactly

in its original place. As the boom echoed out, all he could think of was the madness of PinPin, which had doubtless caused the death of countless loved ones. In rage and anger he pursued PinPin and the stranger, the two careless deserters. He traced the footprints of PinPin and some flat-footed human until eventually he arrived at his village which was empty. Seeing his father's boomerang and a murky outline of someone he continued until he arrived at the cave where all strangers came from.

Then he awoke; he was on top of Uluru.

THE DREAMING EVENT YEAR 39,999

Styles came in for his reading. He was nervous, excited and happy to get the proceedings over with. The explanation of his dreams, were presented as beautiful, full colour artwork. There was a crowd of ten thousand people who were all there because they had all dreamt of this exact moment.

Styles in the general sense was the same as any other blessed Astraliyan and his days were spent like most others, with his life full of awareness. He was a friendly chap and had ways of making life go a certain way. So he knew that he was able to smile at the crowd and with it the world.

A lot of people in different areas of Tjikurpa had been dreaming about a person they had never met – him - Styles. He looked at the 10,000 images of himself and he hardly recognised himself in most of them. He looked distinguished and strong and in many of them he was followed by a red lion, in the others he walked on a red path.

All of the paintings of him appeared night after night in different Kalkatungan's dreams. He resonated throughout most of the Jah Vandeans in front of him -saviour type. To his right were all of his Tjikurpa. Another 10,000 images were all hand picked from Styles's own painting collection. He thought he would never see all the paintings he had painted over his lifetime. Some of them he had not seen in over 10 years.

His paintings included a lot of hairy looking men, others with weapons. The hollow cave was so high the images at the top were hard to see. He wondered if the elders had ever compiled so many paintings together at one time. The collected volume from the real world on the exploits of Styles served as divine instruction and did many things.

The Elder Greyham stepped up slowly, his animal was a turtle, a shell talisman was on the man's back. Greyham pointed to the bottom right hand corner of the wall with the 10,000 images. Styles looked at the paintings, trying to take in as much information as he could, one by one. The first picture was peaceful. There was a large ship inside of which was an S for Styles. Above the shore was a can-garoo looking down at the ship. The next image showed a cangaroo planting a flower near a cliff with a large ship nearby. Then it showed a poison going into the water near the cliff.

The images were a lot to take in. He stood still and stared. Further up the wall was an image of Styles standing near the Ocean; the Vessel is in front of him. On another image he was dressed as a turtle, going on to the Vessel. Over and over on the wall one word is repeated - "HER-SCHEL".

After leaving the Dreaming Ceremony, he had met with the 72 Elders who all agreed that he would take a constant walkabout in attainment of all he should learn before that fateful day should arrive. He was presented to the Magnificent Crystal where he expected to speak to all 6 Kings.

He expected to receive wise counsel. The King of Kulkutan in Vandea Superior issued this message in Sign Language.

"Little brother, as of today Descendants of Zingis are the only ones safe. All tribes of Ameri Can are now classed as animal. Wang Can are classed as animal. Even all the tribe of Cali - the tribe of Hawa Yudah, all descendants of Tolteczus - none now have rights. .

Powah to Hawah

They copied the zodiac constitution with the help of entire Moorabite Men. They have copied our entire history and report it as their own. Hawah, they cannot stop Hawah. You must search for more help. You Can Guru find a way. For your nation, you are the connection to the law. You are the penultimate of your people, find someone in the Dreaming who can help us, all of us."

As the Magnificent Crystal turned to face the next King, Styles looked at the 72 Elders, not one of them seemed to care about what had happened to the people of Meshika and Cali, as if under a trance. He had always wanted to go to Cali.

The next screen blazed on, it was the King of Kalkathunga island Fortess of Vandea Minor.

"We have been issued a new time of 1777 AD. We publicly accept or die, Hawah, the spell is strong, It is no longer the year 40,000, this is our help to you, The children of god are coming to see you big brother, may Hawah be with you.
Hide your Tjikirpa from them, for they will assimilate it"

Styles was then taken away from the screen area, He was not going to see the last 4 kings. Only the 72 Elders would see that. He was led away by Grey Ham and played a song of the sacred twigs on his wind instrument. The song represented a place where he would find aids for his long journey.

He would choose from one of the 6 sacred twigs a talisman left by a king, it would serve as protection on his travels. Everyone in Jah Vah knew where the sacred twigs were. All he understood of this was that there had been no real effort for him on their behalf. They seemed jealous that he of all people could see and they could not. He tried to focus his thoughts on the task at hand. There was nothing else to be done, but follow the dreaming.

An Elder called Uca asked if he would speak to some people who really wanted to speak to him. He obliged. He turned to be greeted by two women around his age, they both said hello in Kalkatuncan sign language, as was custom at ceremonies. They seemed unsure as to speak or not. "No one has left the Tjikurpa, by all means speak" Styles spoke out.

Uca though a professed elder, had failed to properly introduce the two. As Styles looked around he noticed the two flutes in the hands of the women. There were 32 such flutes in existence. These two were two of the 32 Flute Crew of the Peruvian School of music. For 32 thousand years they had successfully passed flute through the ancient urban areas of Chico Norte. They were the eldest peoples of all of the Vandea Superior.

Styles spoke out. He had a few moments to say Shalawam to some people who he had spoken to in Tjikurpa - the dream world, where people communicate. They hugged him, it felt to him like a family and he had never felt so safe as he had in the time he had been here. The two people he spoke two were friendly enough. They laughed about how they had all just had déjà vu. Then one by one, they all looked at each other in wonder, screaming, "Tjikurpa".

The first dreamer he met - Bey Ren Jah gave her best advice.

"Some people said the kings were the ones on the boats in your paintings who had visited centuries earlier and erected the obelisk and ancient cities."

Another called Chy Rel interrupted and said, "No, that was the family of Styles, who had done that", and that "People should not speak of things they do not know about". Styles told them that it was possible either way and it made Bey Ren Jah smile.

"That time had been the same, only then those that came had left returning to a colder climate northwards",

Bey Ren Jah continued with Chy Rel listening.

"Nowadays there was still the odd pyramid here and there but it was the odd boulders all over the country which warped me the most."

Styles was genuinely interested and was about to respond when an Elder appeared and laughing came up behind him. Turning to face him he said, "The enigmas that were explained by word and nothing else".

All fell silent. By the time he left for walkabout, the couple of the dreamers he had befriended convinced him that maybe it was the end of dreamtime. How it would be the horrible end of the Tjikirpa unless he stopped it. He had to somehow convince the people on the boat in his Tjikirpa of the errors that they were to undertake and find someone in the Tjikirpa who had the answer.

LIMESTONE WALKABOUT

The walkabout took him to a sacred place with sitting rocks. Here he was told the high old story of Devils marbles. How the devil had been playing one day with large monolithic round boulders the size of trees. While appearing at sunrise the can-garoo spotted him. The devil left the marbles as they were.

He did not doubt the words of the wise old teacher. He had never seen the devil out. He wondered why he would have pockets. After this trip to the weird place and lonely island he returned to Uluru, the trip had taken two years. When he returned there was no large celebration. They were a year late.

He met a family and learned the continuing history of his future. He entered with his father figure - Nip-Nip. Styles looked at his dreaming pictures with everyone watching too. A large audience of people who he had not met more than once before, all had significant dreams, however, which involved him.

He seemed to be doing the same things in all the encounters, which people had seen. Getting along with people all over the world, whenever a person dreamed of Styles, it was with a shock that the world was changing. The encounters Styles had in the paintings were like he was in a fake land. The clocks were wrong, the days, the numbers, everything was upside down and back to front. His world was becoming a reverse mirror image of itself. Yet somehow Styles was going to stop them - ultimately obliterating their attack.

They would not fight physically. They believed this because he could dream past the year 40,000. Styles' dreams told that he was to leave with these travelers. Once he did, he would lead them to the furthest place possible, gathering more and more. The dreaming never lied. Their people knew other news too; all Styles knew was that he was to leave again. They were also expecting the future maker they knew as Styles to leave soon.

THE BAMBOO AND THE BREW

As Styles celebrated his final days in the area of Uluru there was much to be said but his people were not with him, only his CanFather, NipNip.

He had always known his father, the CanFather, NipNip"It was all possible" frequently seemed to be the words of his CanFather, throughout their life together exploring and learning all the points of Jah Vah. He and his CanFather always saw everything that was to be seen. All the magnificent underground life ways, the surface domes and all the worldly possessions that amounted to the weird and wonderful rock formations, placed across Jah Vah.

Along with the constructs, there were forty millennium of knowledge in the pristine dreaming paintings of all the Jah Vandean and Kalkatun families. The history of the rocks all moved into positions that required nothing to understand.

As the years passed on, in their final walkabout together, Styles had become detached from his father. As Styles was twenty-three years old and nobody consciously knew when he would return from his journey, (not even the CanFather) it was decided he would learn to see colour within colour.

After the ceremonies of the year had passed that night his father took him to Gympie Astraliyah. It was while they were here, they traced some special plants, which were known as teachers and were very sacred. The plants, when brewed in a certain way caused visions of things, which appeared in the air and sometimes disappeared.

Yet the thing that made all find something true, was in the name of these plants – the teachers. The plant when taken correctly, opened peoples eyes to the real wonders of the world. NipNip would say "Soon you will understand if there is anything to learn or are the plants just hallucinogenic dreams with no real meaning to it, let alone reality".

After he took food and enjoyed the sunset, they sat on a long ancient wall that lay near a river. Styles looked closer at what he was sitting on. The wall was one large rect-angled cuboid limestone and there were pictish drawings finely carved in it. It reminded him of the obelisks which stood in Astraliyah. Only this one was lying down in a field as if eased over with force. The river was young and before his mind wondered further, NipNip called Styles.

LIMESTONE PINE

"Styles, it is time. Go! Do anything you must, as in an hour we will surely be occupied". He jumped off the wall and as he did he noticed it was an obelisk, which lay sideways in the grass.

As they ventured away from the river they spoke not a word. NipNip, for measurement did a little tap on the ground with the heels of his feet every second step, as if to say whatever was ahead they would dance through it. They continued north until an hour had passed, climbing and then descending the creek. The familiar animals arrived at the waterhole. Large bamboo type roots grew out of a whole side of the hole. There were birds sitting on a large round, almost oval, pebble, larger than those at the Devils marbles.

Settling in the area for the night, there were a few hours of sunlight left. NipNip chose a smaller stone to sit on and asked Styles to join him. As they sat on the smooth bedrock they looked towards the watering hole and the large bamboo, which dwarfed the long boulder behind it. The bamboo was roughly 20 feet tall, with some laid back as if in a constant blow of wind, others standing directly upright. The sky was clearly light blue.

Styles made a fire, while NipNip prepared the teachers, this would serve as physical as well as mental nourishment. That night Styles stared intently at his father preparing the brew. If Styles' s eyes were to open he did not want to miss a moment of it.

As his father continued to create, Styles looked around his surrounding. It was a peaceful place, which seemed to attract life. There had been vast parts of the journey where they had not seen much activity from the outback. Now they were at a watering hole where all local and far animals passed to taste the nectar like water, which sprang from the ground. Vast rivers flowed all through southern Jah Vah, it was just that most of the rivers were underground.

Yet the knowledge of an earlier time lay with his peoples. This knowledge told where all the rivers used to run above ground. Back when they were expansive roads of rock traversing the scape, now underground and full of water they were used differently. The howl of bamboos from large gusts of wind passed into them becoming the theme song of the evening. The wind had become rhythmic and strange, far too alluring to be mere bamboo.

LIMESTONE BAMBOO

NipNip wondered when he would see his son again. The faith and truth he gave to his son would have to be of great importance and so he tripled the vibrancy in his step, it was his way. They left Gympie square, which was with gold in abundance.

The gold would last for nourishment and only needed to be eaten once. Eating gold was a life choice and because of the dreaming outlook on life it made everything appear more clearly. When they left Gympie they were prepared for the journey ahead. NipNip had acquired raw gold, diamonds and the plant teachers.

Styles had been found lying on a Benben holder. The large monolith tumbled and out of place lying by the river bend seemed almost an island. The larger boulder they came to afterwards, NipNip knew was a chair for the Madagascans as he called them.

The plant teachers had told NipNip to embrace the colours within colours. Just as they had shown him, he prepared the ceremony, Styles blind to what was happening, continued looking at his father's hands to learn the ways of what he was doing.

Oblivious to the wonders in front of him, NipNip hoped all would come to see the truth. Yet, he could not see the optimistic future that Styles had previously embraced concerning his dreams. It was good that Styles was optimistic he thought, but he was sad inside that his son would leave and never return.

How could he return? The elders had specified through the dreaming paintings of thousands of peoples dreams. The last three years had built to this moment and it spelt out that Styles was to leave his CanFather's side.

Styles knew his future, as it had been seen by thousands of people. The Elders and others who also dreamt their future saw no more of Styles after that. He did not return after the change in the perception dream that they had all had, the two and three years previous. No new developments, no new dreams.

NipNip somehow knew he would lose his son and that it was somehow good. The problem was he didn't grasp how losing his son could in fact be a good thing, so he kept motivated for his son's sake. The Dreaming never lied. Besides, he knew ways of talking to his son even if he wasn't there. Soon enough, Styles would learn to do the same.

LIMESTONE THIRD HOUSE

The fire had been going for about enough time, making the area uniformly warm. 'This is how it would begin.' Styles thought to himself. NipNip gave him the hawah brew. He took it to his lips, slowly sipping, "HAWAH!... it tastes like crystal".

NipNip took the didgyriddum and started to play the Dreaming songs. He looked over at the Madagascans, that hopefully Styles would soon see. The sun was setting nicely. There would be an hour before it was gone from view. Styles looked at his father then back down at the brew. He prepared a second cup as he was feeling the need for more influence.

The howl of the bamboo grew more and more until it was in unison with the didgyriddum. The noises were inseparable apart from the faster tempo of the didgyriddum.

PinPin played and Styles listened, it had been about ten minutes or so and Styles thought both NipNip and he had taken enough of the brew for there to be some effects.

As he looked around, he scanned the animals that were at the watering hole. They all continued to drink from water. Behind the watering hole were the large bamboos. He had not seen the tops of the bamboo since staring at the brew for the last five minutes. When he looked up past eye level and towards the top of the bamboo, he grasped what he was looking at.

In the midst of what he saw were eyes unlike anything,

which would make sense. There were massive hands, swollen around the top of one of the bamboos, it was the largest of all the bamboo.

The shoulders and torso outlined the herd of bamboo. The neck and head were monstrously large. The eyes within the mass of the head were huge. The nose was there, but it was not as it should be.

The bamboo went all the way in to the Chiant's mouth distorting the face. In the 3 seconds that had passed since Styles had finally seen the Madagascan, his whole perception of his world changed. It couldn't be real, he thought.

Then he looked at his father, NipNip and the didgyriddum, they looked a lot like the Chiant playing the bamboo, very similar in fact. He noticed PinPin playing and staring directly at the bamboo apex. It was the same one that Styles could see with a Chiant.

NipNip's eyes closed for 3 or 4 seconds at a time. When they finally opened they were focused directly at the eyes of the Chiant. It was like a string connected the Chiants eyes with NipNip. It was in this moment that NipNip stopped playing the didgyriddum. The wind also stopped, along with the bamboo playing Chiant. NipNip turned to Styles and looked him in the eyes.

LIMESTONE LEVIATHORN

NipNip put down the didgyriddum and picked up the brew which gave the drinker second sight. He smiled knowing Styles was now heavily under the influence of the brew. He knew that Styles could see the Madagascans, yet was trying to convince his mind it was not real.

He would eventually accept the truth for what it was, just as he had. He knew that all it would take to convince his son he was looking at Chiants would be a simple acknowledgement. That he too also saw what was making the bamboo howl.

NipNip looked at the Chiant and smiled. The Chiant didn't look back because the Chiant spoke not with words, but with thoughts and feelings. These were beamed straight to NipNip and Styles mistook these communications for his own thoughts.

NipNip continued, "These are the traditions that he had once shown, all what was to be known."

Then his mouth stopped moving. He looked away to the left for a moment then twisted his neck, "HAWAH".

Styles was sure he heard NipNip speak, but saw his face to be still. Then he heard "This is real". The thought was followed by a vision of the Chiant before his eyes.

"This is real - NipNip's face had not moved, so Styles was sure what he had just heard come from behind NipNip. Although the words were telling him other wise they were in NipNip's voice.

Styles focused on NipNip's face and sent a message back with his mind. "Was it real?" NipNip smiled slightly. Nip-Nip focused his entire body so that it was still for a second. Styles thought, "What did he mean?, were the Chiants playing the bamboo real?And was NipNip really talking in his mind?"

"Hawah" he looked at NipNip. He was not speaking but still he heard him. "They are real, the Chiants playing the bamboo, the teachers have shown you."

Styles spoke, "Your lips, they do not move, how do you do this" NipNip only smiled briefly, then again his body went quiet. "Eyes closed, and now open." 'Now do you see?"

Perplexed Styles replied, "Yes but I still don't understand, who are they?, where do they come from? what are they doing here?".

Questions came billowing out of Styles head. NipNip was having a hard time focussing on the important questions.

"They are an elder race, they have always been here. They have great wisdom and can tell us lots about our peoples. Still only the little teachers can show the way, these are not our creator, only creations. You have seen them now and I hope your eyes remain open to see different creations."

LIMESTONE PENSEMENT

Acacia plants were used in cooking and once again Styles saw the Chiants playing the bamboo. The sound was real. He began to understand that the world was even more deep and complex than he could of imagined. The Chiant playing the bamboo so beautifully turned its head for the first time that Styles had noticed.

He shuddered as the thin air in front of him opened up. As all the air behind the Chiant evaporated away, the world behind him appeared. Styles trembled, the world behind the Chiant was beautiful, where large hairy bipedal beasts climbed enormous trees.

Wherever he looked, reality was warped in some way. White spirals of air developing to the right of the bamboos, then large brown feet stepped out of the nothingness. Like from behind a mirror of reality. In doing so the rest of its body materialised, starting with the tips of its long smooth fingers, and a large round mane of hair, It wore a dancing skirt and seemed to be a woman dancing to the music.

As Styles saw the second one dancing freely he received thoughts and feelings, which emanated from the gargantuan. These were a mixture of love and peace which prompted the Chiant to dance as if under a magical spell which neither animal or being would be able to resist.

Styles had heard stories growing up about the Chiants, which once populated the world. NipNip spoke again with his mind "the Chiants had turned away from the good life and embraced a dual way of living. Some Chiants had resisted and it had been because of this that they were still on the Earth. A great flood had drowned most of them long ago. Mankind, which are now 'Children of Hawah' and are treated as such".

Styles knew these creation stories, but never needed to put stock in them until now. Styles was becoming aware of the real and the myth and the imaginary line that was sometimes perceived in the middle. Now he was beginning to understand.

The rest of the week carried on the same way, every night the teachers were used and by the sixth night, six Chiants all of varying sizes had appeared. Different thought projections - long and sad. Others short and happy, passed between the six.

LIMESTONE LONGEVITY

All the feelings, which the Chiants gave off, seemed to spell one of happiness and love. It was a universal love, for the animals, the people, the world and everything in it.

Styles drank a brew, which took four cups to fill and drink. Again the thoughts and feelings he received were the same. It seemed he too was able to talk to his father through pictures and feelings inside his mind. He had heard of the shamans and man teachers with whom he had grown up with using such techniques but again just as with the Chiants he had never had anything which to believe in.

Now it seemed he and his father had no separate thoughts from one another. Styles asked about this connection. NipNip replied, "As a group of children see it rain at the same time therefore share the thought and feeling of it being wet, the same would happen with all the humans on Earth". It seemed everyone had the same mind, the same potential. Yet, everyone had a different location, which ultimately gave each individual a distinct outlook.

Sometimes the deep effect of the teachers made conversation difficult. This mind connection to each reality, made them mirror each other in every way. They were tuned to the natural frequency of the Earth. The plant teachers simply amplified the signal.

Styles suddenly became aware of his fathers sadness at the idea of Styles leaving him. NipNip also became aware that Styles could feel his thoughts and quickly tried to hide his feelings. It worked and Styles began to assume that the powers that he had received were receding. NipNip informed his Can son using words that expressed the feelings his feelings best.

"Soon we will be leaving the Watering hole towards the north, until the big blue water. From then onwards our physical journey together should end. For the Dreaming had said so."

The message was then communicated through thought and feeling to reassure him that the new communication device that they now used, was truly real.

Now more than ever he appreciated his fellow Kalkatungans. More than they could ever know. With all their knowledge about the dreaming and what his own future had in store for him. He knew he would come to miss them all.

A tear came from his eye from staring. NipNip saw the eyes of Styles. He smiled and said

"Find hope in the fact that we can speak with our mind as long as you keep acacia seeds or ever see a Magnificent crystal".

LIMESTONE LEAVING NOW

Weeks passed, continuing north, with Styles conversing with NipNip using thought. Some solemn weeks, with little or no words passing between them. Sometimes a laugh out loud was heard or another by-product of their sophisticated ancient natural form of communication. Styles would point at Mesa's in the distance. Close to these creations he would see large bodies watching him and his father.

Walking across the outback Styles realised that his and his fathers ability to see the ancient ones would probably not wear off.

He was thankful. By the arrival of the new moon Styles and NipNip had made their way across Northern Jah Vandea. Their time together was coming to an end.

NipNip could not see where or how his son would be taken away from him, all he could control was the speed of his walking. The last 50 miles before the ocean were at a snails pace. The final miles took twice as long as normal to reach and when they got to there, NipNip felt as if he had walked too fast. The time with his son had gone by quicker than he had imagined. Soon there would be nothing to say but 'NipNip' and then he would not see his child until the next life.

NipNip thought a lot over the weeks that preceded the final destination, about what he would do with his son in his last few hours. He had envisioned another vision or perhaps fishing, but in the end there was only one thing for him to do.

When they arrived at the final Mesa, which had shaped the route, NipNip did something, which he had not expected. He knew fate would take his son from him, but there was part of him which wanted to control the outcome, some way of winning.

Instead of NipNip leaving his son on the shore like the dreaming had told him to do, he found himself descending the sand dunes and on to the beach. He walked up to the shore and knelt on his left knee in the water. As a tide rushed and washed over him, he closed his eyes and for a moment his mind was cut from the land. His mind raced trying to find a way to stop the crazy Dreaming.

He reappeared. Styles jumped the remnants of the wave. "Since you have not left in the way the Dreaming has said, we will no longer be important in the way their peoples had meant. He ran from the seashore. Styles could not hide his bewilderment. They decided to walk West following the shore.

LIMESTONE CENTRE

At night they slept and for the most part shared the same dream world. They had dreamt of their arrival, approaching an empty beach. It was a solemn dream they both held, and so that afternoon when they arrived at the beach, they were not surprised but both said "Tjikurpa".

The pouch of gold and diamond and acacia seed that Nip-Nip held was getting heavy and they decided to rest for the rest of the day. A stream led to higher ground and so they followed it. As they climbed the grassy hillside above the crack where the stream ran from they found a flat piece of ground, some trees, and a cave entrance. The water was fresh enough to drink and they both took large gulps.

Afterwards NipNip gave Styles something he had never seen before. A small bone bag, it contained fine purple crystal sediment, and gold. The lights were low tonight and only the seven sisters were visible in the night sky.

NipNip gestured with his hands that if he were to 'mix this with the acacia plants, the mixture would make you walk for a month unaided by food or sleep or any other substance.' The conversation then stayed on the matter. "this is an everlasting substance. For a being to use this continually over a long period of time, one would feel the effects of something resembling a young vibrant self.'

Styles eyes widened, as he and NipNip then dabbed their hands in the cloth speckling their paws. "You will be able to see the other world, yet not have the strange effects normally associated with the acacia." Styles asked "How long could one live on nothing but this mixture?".

NipNip replied "Only certain elders who were privy to this exact concoction and techniques for preparing it, we have given you enough to last 7 years, one dab a month will see you through. One must be prepared as much as possible, should you need aid in anyway you must expect not to find it, always prepare, I had had met with other people at the Dreaming events who all wanted to give you gifts and advice. By the end of it all I had became wise among Jah Vandeans. Definitely more advanced than I would have been had my only experience had been, with no feet swelling to dream time paintings."

Styles prepared the fire using a twig rubbing brush technique. "I wonder what will happen, since we have done the opposite of what we were supposed to do. Hawah". Smoke rose from dry grasses on the twigs. "I have prepared myself for death! Or a life of ills for the greater good." He sat back.

He knew he was having moments now where the acacia plants were not having their prescribed effects. Random moments of clarity followed by mild waves of chaos. The blowing of the fire made his head hurt, coupled with the events that were placed out in front of him. He needed some type of closure. What was going to happen to Nip-Nip? He couldn't sense him like he could when they were upon the beach, he no longer heard NipNip's highs and lows.

Was it the purple gold crystal mix? He took advantage of the solemn thinking- unattached from drops from his mentor. He concluded that he ask but one question. He cleared his throat.

"What do we do now that we voluntarily changed the path that we were supposed to cross?"

NipNip smiled but couldn't offer an answer. There was a

long silence.

Crack. A large noise came from within the cave. Echoes shot out, wind blew the twigs. They both turned to see the cave entrance. "Sparkalls" Styles kept on puffing the kindling. "I can see something else." Styles looked up to see the cave now illuminated.

"Trystals within the cave walls" The two of them got up and walked in to the illuminated cave towards the ever-growing lights of the Underground City of Uluru.

THE UNDERGROUND CITY OF ULURU

As the trystals swallowed the darkness encompassing the walls Styles could hear a low buzzing rim. He looked for his reflection in shapes. In the purple reflection which didn't seem to make sense, the pair of them looked animal.

"I am a Can-guru", he said looking at himself, the image now perfect. He was a ruddy brown can-garoo with a large blonde tint.

"Don't get ahead of your self" Styles looked at Nipnip and as he did he smiled, only to see Nipnip also change before him.

"I declare, I see clear when I close my eyes, I see past your face, I see past your disguise, I see past your thoughts and in to your mind." Nipnip traced the floor with his leg which was now covered in hair. "I feel strange," Styles said.

The smell of them had changed, and another smell was on the draft. The scent he could not place gave him a sick feeling.

"Is this what a level up looks like." He said transfixed in his Can-guru self image. Dashes of light were pulsing horizontally within the wall. from his face towards Nipnip and further in to the cave. He reached out with both hands to touch the light and as he did the light flickered then dissolved. Nipnip was making him feel stranger by the second and the lowly cave was beginning to feel like somewhere he had been before.

Shimmering to the right and keeping his hands on the walls, he traced the smoothness until gave it gave way to an opening, a metal of some type wedged in between the blocks which it appeared to be made from. Further across the wall a pink archway could be seen.

He looked back briefly then wandered towards to the archway. Nipnip turned as if to follow and as he did a light came from the floor around him. He shrieked and Styles turned to see the full black and golden Can-garoo stood there. A hairy blackfoot came up and bosh - hitting Styles in the face.

Looking at Nipnip his mind squinted, memories of Nipnip changed. Nipnip had become his alter human form Pinpin, he shouted, "CanFather."

He had not seen for a long time. As he did a second blow came from the riled Can-garoo.

He fell backwards, scraping the walls with panic and fear as he fell back in to the darkness. The glints of purple, evening out, until he stopped falling all together. When he hit the ground he expected it to hurt, but the ground was soft, even though the ground was solid. He felt his skull where he had been kicked, pain hit him. A stinging pain shot through his ribs. He only had mild moments of clarity.

He felt from the floor some type of vibration. He was in a subterranean room. He could not see a way back up. There was a square light coming from a block in the ceiling and he was stood directly under it. Then strange lights came from the walls, which were vastly larger and polygon shaped from top to bottom.

One column as tall as 20 men, lay broken, no longer shining. Its inside crackled reflected silvers and purples. He looked up to where the column had once stood. Sure enough 20 breadths of man up the column space was a light where he must have fell from. No lights were shining up there any more. He could not see the Can-garoo or Nipnip or Pinpin for that matter.

He not how sure how such an enormous trystal had fallen, never the less there it was. As he looked up one last time for Nipnip he knew he would probably need a miracle to be found, unless he found a way down to him.

He last saw the dark smoke and the Can-garoo, a trap maybe, something that reveals enveloping him. He didn't look like he could move. The smoke and the lights were one thing - his face, which was that of Pinpin was something entirely different. His mind raced as to how Nipnip could in fact be Pinpin - the priest king and his ancestor.

The smoke was in the image of Nipnip - the man stood there was Pinpin. In all logical thought the man must be Pinpin. The thoughts being of Nipnip and the buzzing of Pinpin. The spiritual breath against the low buzzing, over and over.

How could his Can Fathers true form be that of someone from long ago, before his birth? The question made his head search for answers. He called out with his mind and then his voice, He received no reply from either channels.

Styles turned around, peaking the glowing hum from the wall across from him, it wasn't moving like the rest of the walls, He walked towards it steadily. He smiled crazily to himself at the looniness of what he was doing. He didn't think he would see Nipnip again, with each step the chances ebbed away. Not just physically but with all that the dreaming had predicted would happen, the nagging smell in his nostrils of Nipnip faded, the intensity of the light heightened the closer he came to the wall. The purple of the crystals within the walls were faded so that he could not see the corridor in front of him. A door way within the wall he thought to himself.

He looked back to the column again - still no sign of Nipnip or the Can-garoo. He took another three steps, four steps, five, he kept counting for safety's sake. Clear across the corridor he reached the opposing walls most luminous point and found another illusion, always a light span horizontally down the walls from his head height further in to the construct, he wasn't sure, but he was sure this place worked with his mind. The corridor curved slowly. Cautiously to step only where the light honoured the walls of purple sapphire construct gave him a much-needed confidence. He had never been a stranger to the darkness but this was different. Matter of fact it was down right bizarre. It was neither dark nor light, just green and purple, everything shone from within itself, the light never really glairing beyond the walls.

The floor began to descend. The thought from Nipnip returned ten fold, sharp pains up the side of head throbbed like a crystal piercing his right temple. The lights got brighter. The corridor straightened. He felt for his head and as he did he became dizzy. He continued to walk almost blinded by the lights all around him.

The pain of not seeing Nipnip again told him to move faster than he would ever in place as sacred as this. As he began to leap faster and faster down the tunnel the light magnified, as did the intensity of the pain. With all his distraught and intent, he echoed out for Nipnip!!!! He thought out to his aforementioned teacher, sadly to no reply. With that the lights dimmed, the distance in the darkness had not been reached. The darkness around Styles began to reach its limit and as it did he saw something, which again made him awe at beautiful construct he was in.

He quickened his pace. Lights began to again throb out of the walls and in to his mind he saw Pinpin maybe 50 feet away. The labyrinth had spit them out on a parallel to a long causeway. (The angle of the light beam above him high up the wall signified more routes higher up). He just needed to move forward and then go round. The he could make his way out. The only way was on to the next one. He pelted forward down the causeway.

Wuump!!! The pain did not subside. Time seemed to slow down. It felt now like he was flying for he could not feel his body. Had drugs kicked in? He was running on pure autonomous motion. He could feel the end of the tunnel, he could feel what lay at the end and he could feel tears trembling upward back in to his eyes.

The feeling of freedom took over him in a way he didn't want to explain. Still his legs went on. The pain continued but it didn't matter, his body didn't matter just the knowledge he could feel coming, the love, the warmth, the pain, it was all coming back to him. The lights began dim again and he opened his eyes to see, but the tears were too much for him to see. His mind was too big to think about just him in this one place. His legs were too strong to give up.

Then, as the lights came on and he had one last thought of Pinpin and his whole being tumbled down the dozen yards of the Causeway. His whole body flopped and slipped the last few yards, until he landed at the place where he had last saw Pinpin. As the pain dissipated and left as quickly as it came, he began to feel as warm as he had been next to the fire. Yet he knew there was no burning flame. He had lost a lot of blood from the Can-garoo kick to the head. It was hard to decipher why he felt like he did. He came to a halt on the floor.

Silence.

He turned his neck, as he lay on there. His back was being toasted by the to the heat source. What was warming him? He lazily looked through one eye. It was a crown of a crystal type. About the same size as his head he thought to himself. Just lying there unknowing. The lights within in reflected from the glowing sapphire tunnel he had just come from. Unlike before there was no pain accompanying it and he half smiled at the crystal as they both lay there in the dirt.

Gazing in to the many crystals that grew from the crown, his face began to glow. He looked at his hands to see the lights, all of the lights. Pretty as they were the crown emanated something that felt he had to touch, the black one. Another was neon red that reminded him of the higher room where Nipnip hopefully still was. He decided to sit up and look around the room to see what was going on. Yet again he was in a place larger than the last.

He stood up and turned around being careful not to touch the crown. He didn't want to talk to whoever was on the other end, especially since they said he was not royal anyway. Almost instantly his thoughts stopped and he did all he could to just breath.

It was not a room he was in. The floor was like a neon frozen sea, as smooth as ice. His eyes were not in sync with his feet or the floor. In the distance a city could be seen. He was underground. As far as he could see. All along the landscape there were lights emitting from what looked like windows - cube, circle and triangle holes cut in to the rock which all emitted lights of different types. Maybe it was a wall. It was like an underground city, surely it went up all the way back to the surface.

To his feet, it was as warm. Still he missed bedrock that danced with sunlight each day between his feet. Between him and the ancient place that he had no deep desire to traverse. In to some underground labyrinth, without Nipnip or was it now Pinpin? He felt strange, the things he thought of could lead anywhere, yet he knew the memories he had too. Maybe in his head he could find a way out of this place. He looked to his left and right as if to prepare himself physically for an onslaught of something un-manifested. He turned and faced left. He looked up and he found the ceiling was perfectly smooth with no exits.

He looked around; he thought to himself - this place is so big that I feel like an ant or a fly inside a Didgeridoo. Then he remembered the story of the Didgeridoo that would be played by an Amerryman who could drink all the waters of the Earth. He lay inside the didge like a small fly.

He turned around to see that the Didgeridoo of Amerry-man continued as far as the eye could see until the horizon could not be seen anymore. The city, with its colourful entrances and outer wall. All of its structure was entirely geometric in design Juts signalling obelisks could be seen.

He looked away as if to assure himself he was alone. He thought to himself "who would be in there? Only familiars or potential summons, with every moment his mind seem to acquire new memory that seemed to have always been there. Waiting here in this place for him.

LIMESTONE REVISITED

He left his mind open to scan the perimeter, seeing if could pick up any thoughts in the distance. The grey landscape in front of him had many entrances, which looked like doors of different sizes and shapes. He wondered how long it could have been there?

Knowing his race of people had lived above ground for the last forty millennia made his eyes squint. The sheer size of the complex in front of him perplexed him. He stepped forward surveying the ground with his eyes, listening with all senses as to know what was to be known. He could hear nothing but the grandeur of the design. He could feel himself being drawn in. The temperature began to fall as he walked away from the crown and toward the megalithic wall entrance in front of him. The wall length was at least a kilometre across. Still in front of him, far off ahead he could see an enormous head, which stood comparatively still whilst looking at him. Watching him.

He walked slowly until he realised he was not hallucinating or seeing an actual creation. The head was made of one large piece of rock. The full round face with some type of animal skin over the head reminded him of Pinpin. As he neared the walls he estimated them to be at least 150 metres high. The causeway lead to the Pinpin headed statue. Again he thought of Pinpin momentarily confusing him as if in a dream. He knew this was no dream though, down here underground trapped off from the human web of energy.

The energy that made the sky appear blue to human eyes, telling Styles that he could be dreaming. As his mind raced to understand why the impossible statue of Pinpin was there, he shuddered to think his life was nothing but a dream. He was able to not only access his early and suppressed memories, but also the memories of others. His thoughts were miniscule in comparison to what he saw in front of him and for every second he walked a thousand questions came to him. Arriving at the entrance to the city he looked at all the thousands of enormous rocks all cut and elevated as if by magic in to place.

The sheer size of even the smallest rock hewn in to the wall defied belief. Stepping forward he saw the path in front of him came to an end. The Chiant head attached to a body that rose up in front of him as he came to a halt. The statue must have stood at least 143 metres tall and about 72 metres broad at the shoulders. At the feet of the behemoth he could see yet more neon lighting. He was curious, but other than jump there was no physical way to get down there.

The Chiant statue had a strap around its wrist as well as round flower in the middle with 12 petals. In its hand was some type mechanical device that seemed to look like a warp whistle. In the other hand was some type of fruit or nut or possibly a pine cone. The Chiant was clothed in golden scales that covered the whole body, except for the face. He tried getting a better view of the back of the head and as he did he saw that the Chiant was clothed in a Chiant fish. The Chiant wore the skin of the fish like a hooded robe. He wondered who was more important, the behemoth or the Leviathan on his back. He saw the face of the statue, thinking of Pinpin he tried to get above ground. If he walked out from the statue, surely he would find his way home.

LIMESTONE BLESSING

He had to return to where he was supposed to be, he had seen enough and he knew that he had overstepped his boundaries. The Face looked passed him towards the Sapphire tunnel where he had came from. He turned around and started walking back the way he came and couldn't help admire the craftsmanship of it all.

The wall still in front of him and its entrance was built at an inclination seemed to penetrate the sky, He knew it to be an optical illusion but just the same he admired it stopping momentarily. The colour of both the wall and the ceiling blended. He knew the wall didn't actually touch the ceiling - it just looked that way.

The path in between two walls twinkled. Where the shadow had arrived inside of the Wall, free from the splattering luminosity of the floor, where it was still dark.

He altered his direction with a pivot of his heal and continued to walk towards the twinkle. The only thought on his mind was whether he would attain experience from the detour. He hoped it could be a fellow Jah Vandean, he needed help, he thought. Then remembered what Styles had said 'Learn to work with nothing' or something like that. He focused as he walked trying to remember what he had been told. He changed his mind too, he wasn't trying to be found by the dreamers.

The polygon faces that made up the floor twinkled. Enough so he saw the outline of the eyes of someone watching him. He pelted out a strong emotion of himself as to show whoever he they were who he was there that he was a dreamer using teachers and was looking for a shaman, unless they had the crown. Had he fucked up. That message would go out to everyone.

There was no reply - only elders who knew how to dissolve themselves in to the rainbow, only one of the 72 elders could hide their presence. He went from thinking it wasn't Nipnip to it must be Pinpin. Even though they were both aspects of the same person. He sent out his own thoughts as messages whilst continuing to walk in thought. As he approached, it became dark and he decided to close his eyes for a moment, adjusting to the darkness.

When he opened them again. He screamed, "Hawah!". Asking for the trystals to come to life. The walls began to lighten up. Within each brick multitudes of pigments brightened to pure yellow. A reflection appeared once more, it was that of , "Pinpin!" He screamed. The trystal yellow walls then glowed fiery purples. Trystals grew quickly reshaping his face to that of himself, Styles. He smiled, then realised it was all just his reflection. Pinpin was not actually there.

The plant like weeds which grew between the bricks adorned the walls reacted to his breath. They themselves were a wondrous creation. Each brick was plated with sapphire. The entire wall was schools of sapphire. The plants somehow grew single bud organic life that resembled Can-Ibis, another of his elders and teachers. The Ibis headed plant had 7 dreads pointing like a star. The pattern was geometric.

Styles hummed the corresponding sound. He knew his hum was that of the image because it was a popular image, everybody knew it. He wondered about the sacred wall. With the super crystal can-ibis looking plant he picked it and put the heavy plant in his bone bag. Then said, "Hawah". His breath affecting the wall before him and gave life to the plant. All around where he had picked, he saw before him roughly 54 pretty spirals growing from the wall. As hard as crystal was supposed to be he had plucked it quite easily. He smiled knowing that in its place were bouquets of smaller doppelgangers.

The flower meant in human expression "patience" or "wait". He touched the wall and made a prayer to be finding his way to a safe Pinpin. As he did he felt and heard a crescendo coming from the other side of the wall. The thundering wallop was loud enough for him to locate the source and then to find his way back out. The sound was like a huge bird... it went higher. He knew the sound would disappear in his underground place. He ran out of the entrance. Surely someone had entered the cave and was making a racket. Crack, another crescendo, it seemed to bang louder and louder, he looked in the direction of where the noise came from, he couldn't see anything that would warrant noise like that.

Running towards the large causeway ahead of him across the flat landscape. He clocked the direction of the bang. He ran to the outline of a purple pathway going up to the sky. Pelting flat out across the purple pathway. The noise – the bang - didn't make sense as sound meant everything to his peoples.

Sounds were made for reasons and if there was a sound which was not understood then it would leave a nagging question behind. Bang, bang, there it was again. This time the noise came again he saw a flash on his right just before the bang. Something was happening from down the tunnel on his right. The enormous tunnel that seemed to stretch forever like a didgeridoo laid out many miles. It must be an illusion he thought. But the bang was real though, and dangerous.

LIMESTONE TRISTE

Within the long ever-lasting tunnel, he could see a light not much unlike the ones growing from the ground around him. To his left was another tunnel, as vast and expansive. Dug out long ago. After surmising the roof of the tunnel to be 200 metres high, he peered on to the right smiling briefly, the lights danced and flickered, happily moving in two small orbits from right to left. He hadn't figured out what that light was. Then as Styles looked at the floor, sparks and a ping nose of something fast flew out. The ground he noticed and the polygons where he stood and others were now yellow. The ones in the distance were not. The two swirling lights, in the distance. How could they not be? He was sure they belonged to the feelings associated with the eyes he saw upon the bamboo that day. The eyes grew large and eclipsed the flashes that had been bellowing below. It was Madagascan. A sense of danger was with it. How might they have appeared in this place?

Boom! With a thump, that shattered his train of thought and the connection with the ancient one in the tunnel. He looked to his left. The icy looking tunnel to his left he saw looked like a man. The figure stood still. In the hands was the crown he had seen. The crown of 36 trystals. The feeling calling him towards the fiery trystals provoked him with each step. To his right, the shadow of the Madagascan seemed to lighten up and become luminescent green and opal purple, deep and thick.

As the man to his left placed the crown upon his head he screamed "Hawah" the man on the right dressed in a dark uniform held a crude gun. Oblivious to the towering Madagascan hovering over him, the two eyes of the Madagascans, were all that Styles could see, even now. It was obvious the human was confused. If he - Styles - had only now discovered Madagascans, then he assumed the human would not see it. For it looked like two yellow moons and as it turned sideways, its purple furry fog was impossible to discern. Trying to read into the poor man's soul, he ran to the man with the crown. He was nervous so he counted his steps. The crown was easy to see, its colours and shines preceded it. If the colours played like that when this person wore the crown then maybe they would help him find a way out.

The man waved putting three middle fingers in the air. 54th step. He looked to his right to see the Madagascan's eyes look up in pain, the human screamed, inhaling the mad essence into his entire being. Suddenly Styles felt terrible, as the pain shuddered inside him, he realised the man with the gun was waiting for him the entire time. Some how he knew the man with the 36 crystal crown. As he ran ever closer to the crowned man he realised the man resembled the statue that lay behind him, the elders, Pinpin.

Waves of memories flowed over him. Flashes of light lit up his face, still he does not blink. He felt the vibrant waves of light with his eyes. The rainbow cycle flared from the crowned crystals illuminating the mans head. Black and obsidian flew his mind to the further reaches of Jah Vah to Jah Can where the feelings ebbed and took hold of all the darkness. Yellow light quartz and quickly counter acted the effects of the otherworldly obsidian.

Styles felt like a symphony of sound. C's G's and he could hear the song of the crown. He could hear Nipnip's words in the air. "The trystals on the crown were from every different place in the world and that the connection between the various kingdoms, where the original trystals were located were al upon this one crown, were all connected to the man who wore it. This would happen in the tjikirpa "dreamworld."

Through the cracks in the light, he saw for the first time what he had wanted to see his whole life, his fathers face. In the crown and upon the face that wore it, was his father. Free from all the can-garoo type qualities he was used to. His father had some how acquired all those years ago. It's you -'Can-Father!!

Styles screamed to the bearded man in front of him using his 'mindbone', cautiously to not alert the human, a kilometre to his right.

The human seemed to be taking his time in doing anything of consequence and had been oblivious to the behemoth Madagascan. The flowers growing from the phosphorous megalithic walls shone white like opal, they were growing to massive proportions. He knew the flower only looked like one and that there was more to see. Then slowly the flowers began to recede back in to the crystal wall as if dying and completing a season in moments.

The human who had been stood still was now absorbing the energies left from the behemoth whether the human knew it or not one day he would be able to summon the powers of that behemoth. As all the light and fear sucked in to the void, only feet from the clothed human. Styles observed carefully using his second sight. The human ran towards to the wall near the statue. Blue light trickled off the human like he had fireflies in his ears. "Do not worry he cannot see us," the man said. He could he feel a lump swelling in his throat and he became thirsty in the first time he could ever remember. Memories of him and his father flew from the blue glow atop his father's head, memories of them together in their place with their people. He could feel an inner sense of responsibility and awareness he hadn't felt in a long time. The bearded man who had been focusing his crystal energies upon the pair of them transgressing memories and instilling wisdom did something unexpected. He turned around and faced away from Styles revealing his back, which was armoured with tattoos in 9 distinct shapes. The black skin Styles remembered was almost un-seeable for the tattoos shone in multiple spectrums of light penetrating every crevice of Pinpin's back. The tattoos were known as the 9.

As the luminescent tattoos became the dominant light source. Styles protected his face with his hands, as he did he saw his hands from another perspective. They looked more like the paws of Nipnip, "so this is what levelling up feels like" he said again, as if to let him Pinpin know everything was okay. The landscape beyond Styles paws shone bright now, it was more magnificent then the changing form of his hands.

The human had made it to the underground city. He could see now this city was where the two colossal tunnels met at obelisks and tubular peaks lay only on the top right portion of constructs. There seemed to be a sky of some type. A greenish fog scuttled across the roof. Purple light would weave between the vapours. The once dead and long forgotten city was alive with activity. Ingenious devices lay harnessing the power of the sun. The human was now gone from view, oblivious to the two of them. He turned around to see the Pinpin, and the crown. Light in the cave was receding all over, from the crown here, he could see the other worldly pictures flowing from the apex of the crown like some projector. Images from within the crystals. It reminded him of the show reel of the Dreaming. It was like the Dreaming everybody saw, only 40,000 years more advanced. The pictures were in motion like the flickering of hair under the close inspection of his eyes.

The rest of the cave however had quietened down almost entirely. The crown was showing him something and it seemed he had the time to take in what was happening.

The symphony of music that accompanied the light show was glory to the ears. The turquoise crystal on the side of the bearded mans head began to whistle high and all of the other lights took a deep creamy green, which electrified the air. The Afro between the crown and Pinpin fluffed up. Waves of moving light projected above Style's head. He was doing his best to concentrate on them; the turquoise was giving him flashbacks. Images of harlequin snakes, the black and white serpents.

Flashbacks of learning with Pinpin, how to throw boomerangs upwards. Excellent when you are in narrow spaces. He had managed to throw the boomerang into a nest of harlequin snakes upon a pyramid in Gympie - or so he thought. The boomerang had came flying and he caught it. He reminisced the exact same images projecting from the apex of the crown never sure which image he had conjured first the one in his head or the one in front of him. Pinpin was not moving on purpose, as if in deep concentration. Sweat upon his brow glowed in the light, a rainbow of sweat on his forehead. He too effected by the slowing of time. Whatever happening attributed to the atacamite stone shining on Pinpin's brow. Then a feeling of weirdness came over Styles, he looked over at the path the human had taken.

He looked back at the city behind him. The ether had made its way down the wall of the mighty pillar entrance, absorbing in to the wall. The glowing wall disappearing under the curtain.

"I see you have your crown" he said to Pinpin.

"Yes. It is done, Go up that way," pointing behind him directly at the causeway.

"It will take you out of here."

"Are you coming?"

"No I'm gonna stay. See what this human is up to. He won't recognise me in this form, I'll only be a while, don't come back in here though, I don't know how long till the Kong Roo comes back." He would return one day to see his father, he hoped. "You must be fast like the boomerang and be gone. - Now go!! Styles Can"

With that thought he ran up the steep Causeway. He looked back towards his father and saw nothing but shaking blue lights never slowing down as he ran. Concentrating on the Sapphire entrance, the half mile of rock glistened every time his heel left the ground. His feet began to glow. He looked down at his feet absorbing resonance. It made for experience. The sound off his feet was affecting the colour of the polygons. At the end of the Causeway he noticed a shining object on the floor. A single silicon flower growing, a round purple bud tranquil. He knew he would take it. He reached out with both hands to take the flower and put it in his hair deep in the middle.

Underneath the flower root was a sapphire disc, it was smooth and as wide as his palm. He picked it up noticing that it was part of the floor. He hadn't noticed before but the whole underground was made of polygons gleaming on the floor.

There was forty thousand years between him and that place, and with that he ran back up to the sapphire place where he had been kicked by the Kong Roo. It would never be destroyed, he thought to himself as he walked past the column that let him fall so easily.

As he looked through the mighty gap where he had fallen he felt dizzy. Stepping back got out he felt his head; there was luminous plant juice and his blood on his hands.

As it mixed he saw through his hands and to the floor. He tried to focus his eyes and it only made things worse. (X-ray vision from trystal plant and blood he thought to himself).

He sat for a moment and looked in the sapphire walls. Taking out the sapphire disk from his hair he compared the two. They were exactly the same material, deep blue and one of the perfect synchronicities through the realms. He was in his element. It was round and solid like the Earth. At first glance a grounding stone he thought. As he left between the smooth colossal sapphire cut rock walls he half expected to see Nipnip stood there smiling. He thought through his memories and realised he had no role models to speak of, none but Nipnip.

For some reason though his only concern was to get out of this place and back to the never-ending limestone bedrock beneath his feet, not over it, left to them by the ancient Madagascan. At least those caves were still a place for them to live until summoned. Styles noticed the campfire was still going. He could see it.

Nipnip had led him to this place and now he was all alone. Leaving the cave he thought blasted Nipnip's name hoping to hear something. Nothing called back. After collecting twigs and brush and putting a healthy portion on the fire, he decided he would meditate in a sleep like state until the last few hours of darkness receded. Hoping, that somehow wherever Nipnip was, he would be okay.

LIMESTONE COLDKILLER

He knew there was a large chance he might not see him again and he became terribly sad. As he lay there next to the fire a tear gathered in his left eye and slid down his cheek trickling in to his ear. No he wouldn't leave me like that he thought, he just wouldn't. Anything could of happened but not that, he told himself.

As he looked out towards the sky he could still see the seven sisters, their lights twinkling. Mentally exhausted from receiving no communication from anyone Styles fell in to a deep sleep. He found himself in a memory full of energy again and walking with intention across a familiar stretch of land. His fathers boomerang stood on the floor in front of him. Dug in to the dirt and protruding outwards.

As he stopped in front of it, he felt the urge to scream for his fathers name. "Father" he shouted with as much power as his lungs could muster. No reply, he felt worried and couldn't think straight. He was worried and felt his belly growl. In the distance he saw something moving on top of what looked like an ancient hill. "Father" he shouted again, the figure on the edge of the terraced hill began to disappear from view. Suddenly a voice as beautiful as sun rays came from behind him.

"Styles". He turned around to see a woman in the distance, he acted like he didn't know who was calling, took the boomerang from the dirt and ran to evade the woman's line of sight. It was weird and almost like he was someone else. "Mother I'll be right back". He shouted then ran through the maze of grass in the direction of the figure now most surely walking down the back of the hill.

As he made his way over, he was just in time to see the figure edge down from view again leaving only the magnificence of the sea in front of him. Running as fast as he could, he made his way to the golden-sanded beach. To his left the beach stretched as far as the eye could see. There were a few rocky outcrops visible on top of the sea occasionally shining with a golden glow. To his right the beach continued up about a thousand steps until a rocky outcrop took over the view, he could see past this point of the beach and decided to run towards it. As he made it to the end he descended the embankment and climbed over the rocks, which had smooth parallel grains in them. It was eroded from the sea and seemed to look out of place here at the sea.

Once on top of the layered stone causeway and with a better view to find the mysterious figure he found the beach to continue on. It stretched as far as the eye could see and there was no one to be found. As he looked back towards land where the rocky outcrop came from and out in to the sea, he saw the embankment rose much higher at this point than anywhere else along the beach. He walked over for a closer look. A series of pebbles placed on top of each other. Some smaller as they reached the top and all seemed to be pointing in one direction, towards the land.

As he looked up he could see a towering cave in front of him. The entrance was semi hidden due to the inclination of the walls and green that hung around the entrance, like his hair did around the side of his face. His face, he felt his hair and remembered that his hair was normally a lot longer than this, about 6 years to be in fact. What had happened to his hair?

LIMESTONE FLASHBACK

He was in a dream unable to differentiate from the events, which had passed previously.

Drifting in to the mouth of the weird looking cave construct he gave one last look at the sparkling ocean. As the path descended he began to glide. A warm rush came over him.

The light warmed his feet. He stopped gliding, marvelling the polygons spiralling the sapphire tunnel. Bright indigos pulsed from his steps like canoe ripples down a river rippling back.

Shining in the middle of the tunnel was a silver line. As he walked to the silver line the boomerang began to act alone. The boomerang in his hand started rising up.

He looked at it. A metallic substance embroidered into the boomerang similar to the line in the tunnel. As he pushes down the boomerang, it repels his hand from the ground. No matter how he tries the boomerang will not touch the floor. He runs side to side in the tunnel with his boomerang in hand. A horizontal silver line in the sides of the tunnel make the boomerang repel him back towards the centre of the tunnel.

With this in mind he mounted the boomerang. Leaning forward and pushing with his foot, he began floating down the tunnel. He put his right foot on the floor to slow his pace and again the tunnel illuminated an indigo to violet ripple down the well of the vast construct. He put his left foot down too and looked so as to have a steady look at the double ripple now making its way round the long tunnel. He pulled down with all his might. The boomerang returned the energy in kind lifting him high up in to the tunnel. He clutched his heels around the boomerang and slowly stood up so that he was surfing. Accelerating as he leaned forward.

The light was fading. He overtook the ripple leaning in to the darkness. After some seconds or so, he climbed down putting his left foot on the floor. The light echoed out once more, as he slipped scraping his knee slightly. The kaleidoscope visual echoed down the tunnel as if his weight was more than just a man. When he looked up couldn't believe his eyes. There were several pairs of eyes lighting up in the darkness. As he approached and then passed them, he realised he had to return. This was dangerous territory. He scraped the ground stirring something breathing heavy. He slowed to a stop. Six pairs of eyes stared at him in terror. One 9 feet tall with a long face pointed, voicing the word "Maw". As the indigo ripple went full time all the creatures came in to the light. Kong-roos of immense stature.

He hoped to run away before any of these Chiants could get hold of him. He felt like he was in their lair, or they were protecting it from someone. He started to sprint, wondering how such an experience had turned in to a nightmare. The last sleeping kong-roo closest to him stood up, wandering about. As it looked at the others to see the danger, it then turned to face Styles. He looked at it in the eyes and it looked back at him. Still he continued to sprint towards it. Holding the boomerang high in the air.

The kong-roo undeterred bounced toward the centre of the tunnel. The other can-garoos were stood around waiting for the large kong-roo protect them. Instinctively Styles threw the boomerang with his left hand directly towards the big bad kong-roo blocking his approaching step. The Kong Roo failed to grasp the boomerang laced with metal going up side his head. It hit it in the nose and then skimmed the eye flying off, the noise it made gave Styles the assumption the kong-roo was startled, hurt or had not felt similar pain.

The can-garoo put up its brawny arms around its face. Styles took his last step towards the Chiant and then swerved left towards the boomerang now in the furthest point from the silver line. The other can-garoos were still advancing the large thin one taking the lead. They all arrived with the Kong Roo just as Styles picked up the boomerang. The large Kong-roo voiced a thunderous "Maw!"

Still sprinting, Styles jumps towards the silver line. Wrapping his heels around the boomerang and once again speeding down the centre of the tunnel. The Can-garoo was loose. His speed was picking up. He doesn't look back. Reaching the end of the tunnel he clears the ramp he had once so graciously passed. As he hit the floor he saw three people.

The first thing, which caught his eye, was the outline of Can-garoo ears on the head of a man. His eye was the ears of one of them. Skin over his head draping down his body. Purple sapphires traced the arms of the can-garoo skin and met the fingers of the man, the man looked like a scary version of his own father, but he could not see his whole face. The second man was white man and wore a Maltese cross, the initials S.A. on his black uniform. He looked very out of place.

He looked at Styles with astonishment. As if he had seen something he was not supposed to. The third wasn't a person it was a kind faced female red can-garoo large like the ones in the crystal cave but more tame. The face was like that of a mother who was seeking her child. The white man with the initials S.A. in the middle, backed away slowly while gazing in to Styles' eyes.

He didn't seem to be bothered about the other two and

began to run away towards the icy tunnel to the right. The man with the can-garoo skin on his head walked closer. Styles wanted to get away from the moment. He tried to run but found he couldn't. His feet were fixed firm and immovable. As if there was something otherworldly about this man with the can-garoo skin. If it were his CanFather surely he would say so. The man lifted the headdress so that his face could be seen.

It was Pinpin, his eyes were dark, he had a vacant look on his face. Suddenly his bloodshot pupils appeared and Styles felt more secure. Still he wanted to leave but his body was frozen.

The man took closer steps towards him. The large red Can-garoo sat down its height still matching Styles. It watched, as Pinpin got closer. Pinpin had been concealing a staff behind his back.

Styles wanted to wake up but found he couldn't. The man looked in his eyes as if to say I know you cant wake up, then he said "I know you cant wake up". Then hit Styles round the head with the staff. Then boom - Styles woke up, there, outside the cave.

LIMESTONE SKIRT

White light beamed in to his eyes. The sound of the sea was roaring in his ears. The tide was coming in. The sun was hot. He took a moment to recollect the dream. As he looked up in the sky, a large bird hovered above. Enjoying the warm air. In that moment he was free, he blinked. He wondered if he would ever work out the meaning of his life. For now he was alone and he hoped to change that.

With a sad face he stood up and decided to get to a communication point. There wasn't one close enough. It was a day's walk if he cut across land, he would have to sleep when he got there. The obelisk was definitely big enough to work. Wherever Nipnip was he would hear him.

Everyone would hear him (but he had no other choice). He was supposed to follow the dreaming. He knew that from as much as he could remember. Life was good he had a lot to be thankful for. He would stay close to the coast. He was hopeful to see the people from the paintings - the humans or foam as they were also known. As the foam is what is carried across the ocean, riding the wave.

Yes he would remain to the dreaming.

He clambered around the red sandstone, being careful not to disturb the blue tongue lizards lying like a carpet ceremoniously between the rocks. The silent ushers of the entrance of the cave were left undisturbed for the most part. The lizards admired Styles as he gracefully climbed to the top of the mighty entrance. He tried to keep eye contact the best he could with the little nippers, for it was better to look the devil in the eye than let him do something behind your back.

As he rose to 30 metres up, his hands grasped on to soft squelching moss and slugs. A good Omen he thought to himself as stood up on top of the mighty cave entrance. He paused for a moment taking in deep breaths, then looked up, revealing the plain ahead of him. The acacia mixed with gold had revitalized him. Clicking his left heel to his right toe. Bouncing forward until his rhythm was steady. He burst into a full on sprint. He thought about doing a dance for the slug, as it would never be able to do the same.

The plain out in front of him, dipped and as he went further in land he came to a dry bed where a solemn cactus grew. He knew the cactus well and stopped in front of it. Kneeling to the ground he took a stick, scraping back the sandy landscape and as he did he looked again at the cactus. The magnificent and solemn peak above what he could only describe as the rainbow road. A smile crept on to his face.

He looked back down at the ground. The soil was damp beneath sand. He picked a straw from the ground nearby. He blew through it and poked it in to the hole water popped through. He put his lips to the floor and sucked two mouthfuls of the water. The base crystals in the cave below him, the nutrients from the water would be immense. He then brushed the ground with his right hand making a can-garoo shape in the sand leaving the straw to represent his intended direction to walk. He thought out to Nipnip, nothing. He knew that it was futile for the world had other plans.

He walked on never slowing for anything. Day turned to night and the stars came out. He wondered at their brilliance. There was something uniform about them. This made him question whether any of it could even be real. The way some stars perfectly positioned between each other, making perfect shapes, which he might mistake for the drawings.

THE WISH TREES OF THE VI KINGS

As he came to the end of the plain, trees began to take hold of the horizon. He knew there would be precautions to be taken if he was to go undisturbed. He detached a long thread camouflaged in his hair. It had a small thunderstone attached to it. Wrapping the dense thread around his left hand, he let the thunderstone hit the floor. Remembering a painting from the Tjikurpa paintings he trod forward. In one motion the stone was swinging round his head in an anti clock wise direction.

If any predators were to step against him he would be ready walking closer and closer to the dark tall Banyan trees. A large howl came out, followed by another, then another, Dingoes. He swerved to the right hoping to hide his smell from the crazy canines. "Grrr". Beside him voices, He slowed his rotations. Sloping off to the right, he manoeuvred away so that he was free to run faster. He had lost the dingoes and now grass met the sand again. The view of the stars was his respite once again. The large mile wide beach stretched for miles.

As early sunlight arrived he went inland to the woods again, to the sacred trees. The woods were wide and long. After an hour of navigating through brush and spike he arrived at an open track with large Banyan trees on either side.

The twigs were sacred because of where they grew. There were designs on the trees. The insides were hollowed out long ago, and then fitted with a bark hatch, able to store all manner of items. As his top ranking entitled to choose from the Sacred Twigs. He told himself he was saving the people. Eventually coming to a large can-garoo sign cut in to one of trees. Etchings of a Pinpin - like the one he drew near the cactus, mounted above the rainbow road. He fiddled with the outline of the intricately designed hatch; it was also a perfect shield. The detail of a warrior as he launched a spear in to the distance was epic; on the next frieze the man was in a field, in the next a can-garoo.

On the last was a copper coloured man, with the youthful face of Pinpin. At bottom of the shield three grooves gave him enough grip to lift the shield up and lift up and then to the left. It came out silently and he placed on the floor. Inside the tree on the bottom was a box made of reeds. The box reminded him of the one his aunt had made over and over again showing his cousin the technique. That was a long time ago. The dreaming process for him had distanced him from that life so far long ago, it was hard to remember before that he didn't need to and so he didn't. Still it was hard to not think of the Kalkatuncan people. His cousins even spoke the same sign language. His mother had spoken it for some time when he was younger, spending months speaking only in a sign language. His cousin had taught him the language during that period.

On the floor next to the box was a silver glove and a pouch. A silver chain connected them. It had belonged to Pinpin and now it belonged to him. He picked it up. The pouch was not empty. Eager to see his gift he immediately jumped back, catching his hair on the inside of the tree. The pouch was full of crystals, all small and of varying colours. It looked like a full set. Reaching back in to the wish tree he opened the reed box to find a turrubunga. Inside were 5 perfectly cut stones. Each being large enough to fit in the palm of his hand. He put the turrubunga over his shoulder. Then he slotted the hatch shield back on to the banyan. So all looked how it had before he had arrived.

LIMESTONE FOREVER

He continued to walk between the parallel line of trees as the wind blew through the leaves.

The hatch on the last tree on the right side was shaped like a turtle's shell finished with of blue and gold etching. Drawn to it, he took the turtle shield from the tree and marvelled at it. There was a handle on the back .He twisted it back and forth watching it spin. The turtle would protect him thought.

The sun was high in the sky, still it hard to peer in to the darkness of the tree. He put his right arm in tracing the interior with his hand. There was a lot of sand and another dilly bag made of twisted bark fibres. Pulling it out he found it heavy. His heart started beating fast. Opening it he found it was full of a fine golden white powder.

He dabbed his finger in the material for a taste. He put on the silver glove and poured the crystals from the connected pouch on to the floor. As he did, he noticed one had been shaped in to a blue sapphire ring. He put it on his right hand. Then, putting the crystals in a line he counted thirty six. A full set. He could communicate with them in ways most people could only dream. Satisfied, he scooped white gold in to the pouch. Then put the crystals back in the pouch one by one using the silver glove.

Relying on *déjà vu* he continued to walk. The end of the wish trees brought with it another rise in terrain. This reminded him he still had the vitality of a small hurricane. Sacred hills peppered the region, all spaced perfectly apart, as if someone had placed each grain in to the ground one by one. He felt his dreams of the future bleeding through to reality. Ascending in the same direction he eventually came to flat ground high up on the plateau. Thee wind howled and the sun shone unforgivingly. Still he jogged along the long plateau, with his dilly bag cluttering his back as he did so.

THE CANCEPTION OF TWO BLADES

In the distance a spike towered above all else. From where it was it looked like a tower in the ocean. It was in fact on land and much smaller. As he arrived closer still he found it was an Obelisk, solemn and towering over his head. It must have been 25 feet high. A grass ring surrounded it, with a cliff behind it and with it the ocean.

A weapon lay fixed on the monument - a bronze sword. The blade was straight and the end was sharp. The hilt was of a beautiful shiny black substance, yellow dots set in the grip like an animals spotted fur. As he reached up to take the sword, he felt something reaching for his pockets. The silver glove that had hung at his side was repelled by the sword. There were many stones and woods and metals that had these qualities but only the glove had noticed the sword.

As he unhooked the sword gripping it and admiring the craftsmanship he heard a rumbling high up in the sky. He raised the sword in the air, the weight bought the tip down to the ground. He then looked at the hilt where there were indentations and two precious stones had been laid in. He placed the sword down on the ground. Then put the two dilly bags down and sat down. Then he began to speak out within his mind to Nipnip.

At that exact moment a voice replied. Yelling out from behind the obelisk. Intrigued he followed the voice to the cliff behind the Obelisk. He peered his head over the drop.

To his surprise bobbing in the ocean below a vessel with white sails.

LIMESTONE EDGE

Wind blew knocking him for a second. His brow sweated at the thought of falling to a grisly death. The grains of sand stuck in his eye. The crumbling edge trickled towards the vessel below. By the time he had regained his footing he was almost over the edge. He looked down again at the creation of wood and sweat.

Down in the natural harbour the ship floated to and fro. He looked up and down the deck to see if he could see any humans. There were none in sight and he wondered why that was. Surely he would get a look at one, just to satisfy his curiosity. Just so he knew what he was up against. There were 6 sails.

One of the doors opened on the vessel. A man came out of the cabin dragging what looked to be a human wrapped in a blood soaked cloth sheets. The man stopped for a moment and looked up wiping his brow. Styles popped his back away from the edge. Moments later he heard the sound of a human hitting the water.

Styles slowly put his head back over the edge. The man was nowhere in sight. There were large ripples where something had hit the water. Blood of foam of the sea he thought to himself. Just underneath the water bubbles made their way to the surface marking the spot. All he could see was an open deck. He looked back at the obelisk. It shadowed him. Thinking back to the paintings at the Dreaming Event. There had been a ship. There had also been a can-garoo. Did the Dreaming intend he see Nipnip again? He was full of hope for some reason. *Déjà vu* again flooded through him. He cried "Hawah" then he lifted the sword from floor.

A noise came from over the hill further along the cliff side. That path led down to the natural harbour. Taking the shield over his shoulder, in one hand the didgeridoo and the two dilly bags, with the other holding the sword. He looked like a warrior ready for battle. He believed in himself with all he knew and braced for what was to come over the hill.

The crystals were in his ever-moving pouch and various teacher plants, seeds, material and diamonds were stashed within the didgeridoo. An unlikely place to look. The sapphire disk was woven within his woollen wavy hair. He could feel the elements in the air. Only the thunderstone revealed his intentions.

He could clearly see six men. All broad shouldered and clothed like Moors. One stopped walking abruptly. Retrieving a periscope from a satchel, pointed it in his direction.

The others spread out taking aggressive stances. Were they going to ambush a blind person? Instinctively Styles dropped the sword and the didgeridoo. Thunderstone in hand he swung the thread round his head. A loud shot went off from the human on the left.

Screaming "Hiyaah" The man knelt down to aim at him with a rifle. The ground in front of Styles sparked. The rifleman then turned to speak to his comrade. Rounding the rock, Styles hit the man in the temple. Wasting no time he pulled the stone back using acrobatics to increase momentum. Hitting him square on the forehead. Two down. The other four fired shots. In one last instant he grabbed all he could, namely the Didgeridoo and the shield.

They chased him to the cliff side of the obelisk. One took the way he would escape. The other watched Styles, the third seemed to be interested in the shiny sword and picked it up, the fourth walked over to the bag of golden material. Thankfully Styles had his dilly bags. The Moor grabbed it angrily and threw it over the cliff as if it was a bag of rice.

Styles could only think of one ending. The humans had to calm down. Be humble. He put the shield down at his side and walked toward them. The One with the sword started slapping the back of it against his shoulder. The One blocking his exit looked over the cliff down towards the ship. Styles stopped walking towards the man with the sword. He knelt down and muttered, "Hawah" under his breath.

Opening his eyes he looked upon a blade of grass and whispered his holy intention. Just as he did the lonely cloud in front of the sun darkened the sky. Almost instantly a flash of light came from the sky blinding all eyes, followed by a thunderous noise. Deafening those with ears. The noise rang for miles around. Everyone opened their eyes to find that one of them was no more.

The lightning from the sky took him and all was left was an ashy mess, the three men turned away in terror, thinking they had scene an act of their god. Styles stood there. He was unsure what to do an so he stood there staring at the cloud covered sun. In this moment he realised he must be on the right path.

As cloud moved across the sky changing shape as it went, a lone capped man came from over the hill. The man wore a white shirt and brown trousers. He did not look up all the while he walked. The men he had electrified with his question to the grass were 100 steps away.

The man decided to look up, but only at the obelisk. Then, standing ten feet from him, he turned to Styles. .In a deep voice he said, "Styles, Etsig Can." Styles looked back up at him it was the face of a human. His face was pink from the sun. Clothes to hide their minds. Like there was no mind. The body was all that there was. The man looked back at his hands. He had his mothers dancing skirt from Tasmania.

"Styles", the man said again. Styles looked at the man with disbelief, he asked him from his mind. "Styles" then gave the skirt to him. Styles had not moved since the light, which had came down. He took the Tasmanian skirt and looked at it. The tiger teeth on it polished like they had been. He looked up at the man. Then he saw the man's face for the first time. The one who ran away and left him with the can-garoo and the animal shaman.

The man pulled out a piece of bark that was stuffed in to the back of his shirt. The bark had writing on it and drawings. The picture showed a can-garoo and a boat.

"Styles". He said. Styles who didn't know how or why but responded. He was surprised by the man's broad vocabulary. "Styles I am Senior Almeida, I met you a long time ago, do you remember?"

Styles couldn't remember jack and there was a silence. Senior Almeida was speaking Kalkatungan. The words made him sweat and his brain configured responses. "AL-MEIDA". He said.

"Yes Almeida, we must leave this place Styles, we must go now".

The words echoed through him, they were of urgency. "You are not Jah Vandean!?" Styles asked. The man Senior Almeida pointed at himself and said,

"I am a not Jah Vandean". Then Styles looked around at the single ashy fault where the man who wanted to hurt him had been. His ashes scattered in the breeze. Almeida began to sweat,

"Just my men". He said in a high tone of voice.

"But you my boy. You are the quest.. I will explain all but first we must leave". Styles thought of the dreaming, and all the signs. The constant *déjà vu*. He decided it was best go with him as the dreaming intended. The two of them walked together back towards the hill. Styles stopped for a second as he saw a harlequin snake popping its head out from beneath the protection of the grass. As if investigating what had caused so much ruckus yet brought no supper.

In his best Kalkatungan Styles asked, "What now ?"

"Now we get on the Vessel."

"How can I speak like you?".

"I will explain once we are on the vessel. I will say this there are things that you can do that I cannot, be patient, first I have to handle my crew, there may be one or two members who may see you alive as a problem. They are under orders... of the Dum Diversas 1452. First I will secure you aboard my ship. Then I will explain everything".

"Okay, and where do we go?" Styles asked inquisitively. Senior Almeida responded slowly.

"West and then North. Far from here."

"Let Us Go Den" he said. Six men ran towards them. Then seeing Almeida stopped. In Portuguese the man shouted. Afraid to go any closer. "He! With the thunderbolt from the sky. We witnessed it. He must perish. As the dum Diverses decrees." Almeida looked at Styles. Speaking again in Kalkatungan,"Follow me"..

It was a strange walk. They all stood patiently looking at Styles in the face. The opposite of how Senior Almeida had presented himself. He followed Almeida's lead, who had greeted the largest of the men with a handshake.

The man was red in the face and had red hair. He had broad shoulders and wore a rubber armour that covered his whole body. He wore an armoured fibrous boot. The man must have really needed protecting. The armoured man put on a glove on and walked towards the sword that lay near ignoring the scorched ground.

Once he had the sword he began to walk towards the other 5 men. . At that moment all the crew started shouting in Portuguese. "Dont bring that here" they cried. Almeida walked towards his man in dark armour. He stopped in front of him and turned to Styles. The crew all stopped barking and watched as Almeida spoke Kalkatungan. "Styles! Come here one moment" The Portuguese five all watched. Styles walked over to Almeida and the Redman.

The five began to look at the sky for irregularities. Some squinting at the sun. Others worried beyond belief for men as this dressed in there crosses. As he came closer the two looked at him,

"Styles I introduce to you Sawyer" He bowed Styles did the same.

"You are to make sure nothing happens to the boy here. The seas have shown us much today and I fear the day is not quite yet done. Make it count, none of them can return to the Vessel, I will take the saint here back to the Ship."

Almeida put his right arm over his shoulder and walked him away. Sawyer looked at Styles like he was going to do something bad to him. They walked along the cliff edge. Sawyer shouted to the crewmembers to come closer speaking American. Talking about the obelisk and such.

"Gather round, for we have found
A truly fine resting place
For this disdainful dum diversus
For who of you would stand as strong
As this Obelisk you all see
If the roles were reversed?.
Just how cursed

A twisted bunch we would be"

As they got closer, he lowered the sword to the floor. Straightening his arm he leaned on in resting on it in the sun. All was quiet. Styles looked back only to see the change in Sawyer. The men had no idea what was to happen next.

The point of the sword rose to the closest mans throat. In a single side step he swung down the blade on the second man's arm slicing between his fingers down to the elbow, He had stupidly raised his arm for protection. The other two began further into Jah Vah. To Styles they knew all too well how efficient a killer the man Sawyer was.

The man with one split arm split fell back on the floor, taking in the moment. Sawyer threw the sword at the running men. One of them stopped as it stuck in the ground in front of him. Then deciding against picking it up ran clear up the bank. Running as fast as his leg's could carry him. The other seeing no exit returned begging from his life to Senior Almeida in his best Maltese.

"Senior Almeida, why ? What must I do ? I will not perish like the rest, please, If it is secrecy you want, then I swear to never speak of what you are. Please!".

Senior Almeida ignored him. Sawyer grabbed the man begging man by the eyes and hair. Pulling him to the cliff edge. The man elbowed Sawyer in he nose more than once. Sawyer broke the man's arm.

Then as the man screamed out there was a moment when the man knew he was to die. The man held on to Sawyer with all he could muster.

The man who had one arm sliced began to get up and walk away but fell down when the pain. His arm split in two and hung about he screamed in pain. With that Sawyer released the other's grip and kicked him from the cliff. The man fell to the rocky ending. Not even making it to the ocean.

He then went back and finished off the other dripping man with a kick in the throat. The man with a sliced arm would surely bleed out. He stomped up the hill towards the sword. Then he returned and beheaded the man who screamed in pain about his arm. He jogged back towards Almeida and Styles. He was about 100 steps away when he saw the fourth man galloping down the steep sandy embankment to the left towards Styles and Almeida. All he could do was warn them. "AL MAY DA Your left. Almeida, Almeida your left point !"

Almeida turned to his left just as the man jumped off the precipice down to Almeida. He had a knife and managed to stick it in the forearm of Almeida cutting through the sleeve. Almeida's waved his hands in the air. The man landed on the ground just as Styles turned around. Styles dropped his didgeridoo and ran at the man with his shield. The impact sent the knife into the man's chest knocking him to the floor. Styles, turning to face him as an acrobat would.

The knife had sliced the man's throat. The man had not noticed. He stood up, trying to not look embarrassed in battle. It didn't look too bad. A thin line of red swept across the man's neck. The more Styles looked at the neck the more it bled, so he looked away. The man coughed, more blood trickled from his throat, then blood spurted out and he coughed uncontrollably. All violence leaving his thoughts, he then looked at Sawyer, then Almeida and then Styles. He then fell back sideways on the floor staring at the ocean, mumbling doom.

Almeida was bleeding. Sawyer reached in his pocket and removed a tissue applying pressure to his arm.

"It's fine, its fine, let's get back. Is it done?," looking at Sawyer.

"Yes it is done," he replied.

"Fine." Almedia said. Then they walked on. Styles knew the

silence was to see if Sawyer had not killed anyone. The descending rocky landscape led to a small boat. - their transport off the shore to the Vessel around the bay.

LIMESTONE GOOD BYE

The water was calm and soon the boat was away from the shore dwindling along to a double beat as the water slapped against the shore. The sea was open and warm. The right rocky shore vaulted up the cliffside. Then Styles saw the Vessel again.

Harboured under the rock cliff and he now saw it in all its beauty, 100 foot long, prow sticking out. When he arrived on top he saw how large the whole vessel was. The starboard shone golden. He couldnt see anyone. To his right a large arched cabin. In side he could see a large wheel. To his left there was a small deck at front. It all looked quiet. Almeida was quick to comfort in his best Kalkatungan. "Styles may I introduce to you the Vessel, it is the best ship for what must be done. Come I have much to show you."

Then turning to Sawyer and in English "Retire below and soon we set sail"

"Styles follow me." Styles understood even though it was not Kalkatungan, he was to follow Almeida.

The three of them entered the cabin and opened a trapdoor which led to a spiral staircase. One by one Almeida first and then Styles followed by Sawyer. People could he heard talking. Sawyer shut the trapdoor which made a noise as he slammed it. The sound of people rushing about could be heard.

Above the ship on top of the cliff where the lone monument stood a knowing intelligence looks at the ground and all the men lying there. Jumping closer and closer to the cliff edge he looks over past the can-garoo feet and the sandy cliff edge towards the Vessel below.

VESSEL MA VESSEL

The interior of the Vessel was blue. Light blue tapestries hung from the high walls. The blue walls merely backdrops to the finger like tapestries, which continued to the walkway. The first step was on a blue dragon carpet. The single piece stretched the length of the hallway. The confortable feeling under his bare foot was un-measurable. It accompanied him all the way down the hall. The hall was long. it was like a modified cargo hold. The others grimly walked down to the hall.

About 60 feet down the corridor Sawyer entered a room. Above it read 'ARMORITES'. Styles felt uneasy. Senior Almeida escorted Styles further down the hall to a room door that read 'Living Quarters'.

In his best Kalkatungan he said to Styles. "This is where you'll stay". Then they continued down the hall. A sturdy oak door read 'Almeida Quarters. Hanging from the walls were musical instruments made from metal. As the boat rocked stationary instruments came to life. Clanking back and forth, the Tinsha bells and gong. Styles went around the room slowly looking at the instruments. Another door led to a lab containing stove pots and other vital kitchen crockery. Most hung from the ceiling.

"Ill show you the stock room another time, its in one of the living quarters that we don't use. I can tutor you there. As I am Senior on this Vessel, my living quarters is out of bounds. However, I shall show you around as it is your first time here." With that they spiralled up the second staircase. Styles realised now his eyes were accustomed to the light. An eerie violin was playing somewhere.

The staircase looked like the vertebrate of a giant extinct animal... 16 steps, rising to another trap door leading to the Captain's quarters with more blue walls. The man really liked the ocean. There was a large desk on the left, on the right were two large pictures hanging on the walls. One of the pictures looked a fish scaled big headed man hunting a large dog faced man. He counted 9 tails. He smiled, it reminded him of Nipnip. Then he squinted seeing the predicament the dog-headed man was in. Without saying a word he looked at the rest of the painting. The hunter was man with a fish tail. He was looking back over his shoulder directly at Styles.

The second picture was similar to the last one but less detail, almost all of the dog's head was replaced with blue and the hunter's head was completely separate from the body. Only the thigh to the ankle was visible and there was no fish tail. It was beautiful yet strange, unfinished he thought.

Below these two pictures were three rows of books of varying thicknesses. On the left of the desk sitting in the dark corner of the room was as a large crystal in a star shape. It was mounted on a tripod and the shape had over a hundred sides. It was more or less round and similar to the four stones he had with him, only if you added all the sides together it would create a unified shape.

There was large dresser, a vault, and a bed. There was a small window to the back of the cabin, which gave a view from the back of the Vessel. Then they left through Almeida deck door taking him to the navigation room. The wheel was large and was slotted on top of a metal rod. In the wheel, there were beautifully carved designs, which by Styles estimated took about 500 hours to finish. Carved into a plaque of gold above the wheel read a sign 'Fortunae',

"This wheel shows the creation of all life." Styles gave a look of amusement at the trinket of dubious information. For he knew it to be a lie.

The first showed dog headed ancestral figure, much like, if not the same as, the painting in the Captains quarters. "This our god, he is the son of God, we call him St Christopher."

The first quarter shows our ancestors the Yamna and our ancestral home". The second showed an abyss of pit people. All with their faces searching the floor.
"This is our exodus."
The third quarter showed the ancient Yamna humans leaving caves. Then there was just a symbol – a symbol they wouldn't know to have - a cross. It seemed to tell the story of man in a very crude fashion. For Styles knew it was not his story. That's all he knew. The history of Almeida and Sawyer was another story. But now he was beginning to wonder where they had came from

And what stories inspired Sawyer to carve such a relief. They then went to the starboard bow and spoke for a moment looking out towards the ocean. Styles could feel Astraliyah disappearing the more he learnt. He again wondered about Nipnip who could have been anywhere. Almeida said, "Is everything alright?". Styles changed the subject on him.

"Where are the oars?"

"This is a sailing ship. We just rely on the wind, once the crew turns up, we will have much to discuss!"

Styles looked up at the cliff. as he did he saw some cloth hanging from the birds net on the Vessel. The bag of white gold that had been thrown off the cliff. There was rip in it but there was clearly some weight to it. "Excuse me Almeida", Almeida stood back and watched worriedly. Styles put down his affairs for the first time since meeting Almeida. As he climbed the pole higher and higher Almeida eventually cottoned on to what Styles was doing and began motivating him.

"Just a little further, that's it". Someone Almeida shouted. The next moment Styles was hanging, dropping and swinging until he was back on the deck.. "What's that you got there" Almeida asked

"One of your men took it from me, up there", he pointed to the cliff above. He showed Almeida the bag of powdered 2d gold.

"Its my food".

Food?" He asked.

"Yes special food I make." he then opened the bag and offered Almeida some as if it was merely a cooked potato chip.

Almeida couldn't believe his eyes as he looked in the bag. "But this is, this is, do you know what this is?"

Almeida didn't dare touch it for of irreversible effects. He marvelled at the bag of wisdom then slowly stepped back and a sad frown overcame his face. "What is the matter?" Styles asked.

Almeida didn't reply, instead he shouted for Sawyer who arrived a few moments later dressed in brown boots, brown trousers and a stained white shirt with a thread cord neck.

"Yes Almeida what is it".

"See to it that the new crew are set up and prepare to set sail tonight." Almeida and Styles headed back to the Captains Quarters.

"Styles I can not make the memories you have lost return. That is beyond my means. I can tell you all I know and hope you will understand. This is a map of the world and this is where we are"

Almeida pointed to the painting on the right.

"The last time I came here you were younger and I had travelled from a far away place from here"

Almeida pointed to the top of the painting. "Back then, I led an expedition through the tunnels from the north which brought me here"
Pointing to the bottom of the map.

To Styles "the map" as Almeida called it seemed very weird.

Why is the map upside down? He thought to himself. Almeida continued to ramble on about where he had came from and all the things he had done to reach him. It was a lengthy explanation that Styles found hard to understand and keep up with. Almeida had obviously thought long and hard about what he would say to Styles and now here he was. Styles didn't need to listen to Almeida to know what he had been through all he had to do was relax and focus upon Almeida, then the truth would more or less flow forth. As he did he concentrated on Almeida and all he was saying all of a sudden the memories came flooding back.

The images were vivid and real, he could almost smell his people who had done so much for him. The Dreaming events that followed he already remembered well, because of chasing Pinpin he had found the underground tunnel with its floating strip of silver and his father accompanied by the human and a can-garoo . Then what happened next he could not remember before, the man he saw as his father came closer to him and put him in a deep trance. He was asked to eat something he knew was not normal food and then he was told he would forget all that he had saw. He then remembered passing out and waking in the pouch of an enormous can-garoo. The can-garoo had taken him back to his village where most of the locals were now all working and going about their normal affairs.

It all felt dreamy and he remembered having no desire for anything, he was just kind of numb all over. Even his mother was acting strange. As he arrived on the village a small congregation surrounded him, mostly his friends of the same age. One girl who he thought was his cousin though he had no memory of asked him where he had been? And does he know what he had done? She was hurried away quickly by one of the elders who looked at the can-garoo with an acknowledgement you would normally only reserve for chiefs or Shamans.

The girl continued to scream about something like 'that's not right' and 'where are you taking me', Styles remembered thinking hey what are you doing with her, and then a feeling of passiveness coming over him, the likes of which he had not felt before. It was almost as if it wasn't him stood there but someone else. A shadow even who had all his thoughts and memories yet no desire to do anything.

Over the next few weeks the can-garoo hung around the village, mostly prancing the outskirts of the village picking berries and such. At night the can-garoo would disappear from view and always return the next morning. Styles became good friends with it and again never questioned why he had such an affinity for it. It was weird now when he thought about it.

The can-garoo had a pouch so was obviously female but Styles was sure it was his father. The way the can-garoo followed him, guarded him you couldn't help think such a thing. One night after supper he saw the can-garoo leave the tent of an elder, Thinking back it was a strange time. Not only did he think everything to be normal, no one ever mentioned the incident with Uluru.

The weirdness continued until one day Edgus, the Elder of the village, called Styles into a tent. Edgus who was thoroughly respected for being wise as well as fair told Styles that would commence his walkabout again. This was when the can-guru spoke for the first time giving his name 'Nipnip'. The can-guru seemed to understand direct speech yet always replied with the same answer, "Nipnip" In the tent the elder gave Styles a warm sickly brew to drink and afterwards was told the how one day he would be called to do something great and that when the time come he would return, until then he must leave and stay away from Uluru.

The next six years Styles spent with can- learning and travelling never questioning once why he would do all things with a can-guru. In all those six years he had never once thought about his mother, his father or what had happened at Uluru.

"I remember" Styles said to Senior Almeida giving him a wide-eyed look leaning his head slightly. He knew Almeida wasn't sure and said. "Uluru we opened the door, our people were leaving to escape your peoples arrival. The two worlds could never mix and you, and my father. You interrupted it. My father dropped his drum. I followed him to the cave and then my mother followed too. The pebble fell and the door closed. Almeida watched as Styles recovered all his speech.

"I met you when I was a child, I remember you now, with my father and my mother."

Almeida's eyes fogged up, eyes squinting. Suddenly, a tap at the door. It was Sawyer the crew had arrived and were due to set sail. Almeida excused himself from Styles' company and left Styles in the quarters by himself.

"Look around the ship by all means I'll be on deck."

Considering the arrival of the rest of the crew and all it would lead to, Styles suddenly felt an urge to make the world smaller once again. It wasn't that he couldn't handle whatever lay ahead of him, but surely he must of pondered how alone he would come to be. With that he went lower deck again to find the black man known as Balam. As he returned to the living quarters he wondered where Balam was from? How would they communicate? Why was he there on the boat? As he entered the room he found Balam sat in a seated position, legs crossed with a book reading it patiently. The man had long curly hair and a dark round face. He immediately noticed that they had more or less the same complexion.

The room was lit from a window behind Balam and he was using it to further appreciate the text on the page. Below the window was a large canvas, there were various colours woven into it. It seemed to be a picture of Balam as they both had the same facial features. Balam's feet were long and wide, long strong legs accustomed to walking great distances and quizzical eyes to survey the surroundings. On looking at the picture a second time and then back at the reader, he realised it must be a relation of his, or whoever had painted it, to be a likeness of Balam, they had almost succeeded if it were not for the eyes. Balam's eyes were not as fierce to look at. The muse of the painting was without fear or hate, yet they both looked wise and strong, this troubled Styles. Still the man read his book turning the pages, which contained black writing and pictures.

He took a place in front of him sitting on the floor with his legs crossed placing his affairs beside him. Balam who was not entirely void of conversation began to raise his neck very slowly and his lips began to mumble incoherently. Then he closed the book and looked up at Styles for the first totally focussing on his face. Styles wrinkled the corner of his face in acknowledgement and Balam squinted both of his eyes as they readjusted to the light in front of his forehead towards the ground.

Styles wove his hand up in a circle across his chest and then slowly closed his hand bringing his elbow back down to his waist. Balam watched and at first, hesitated and then responded by raising his hand so that his palm faced Styles. The two of them continued to exchange pleasantries and customs. As the signals were exchanged it became apparent that they shared a source language of Sign.

Styles was using the nationally and most ancient form

of sign language he knew, the signs were basic, but they were known throughout all the tribes in Greater Vandea. Styles asked what Balam's people were called who taught him using a sign that expressed both voice and family. Balam then voiced the word. "Kulkutan" and then "Toltec", shocked by this Styles tilted his head back in astonishment.

He then waited for and then confirmed what Balam had just said, he pointed at Balam and voiced the word back to him. "Kulkutan", Balam smiled in acknowledgement then pointed at Styles and asking the same question using the sign that meant both voice and family. Styles raised an eyebrow and then proudly said "Kalkutun" meaning Greater Dragon.

Balam who was equally as shocked at the answer tilted his head back like Styles had. He then repeated the word back to him. "Kalkutun", Styles smiled and nodded. Then pointed at Balam and said the two very similar words. "KUL-KU-TAN" pointing at Balam then "KAL-KU-TUN". The words were so similarly sounding and the fact that their sign language share common based signs, led the two of them almost instantly to believe that they were in fact distant cousins. They both smiled and then hugged. It felt good for both of them.

Balam then opened his book again and showed Styles a page with a large picture of snake on it.
Balam pointed at it and said "Kulkutan" and then pointed at the sky, Styles felt like his brain was melting the snake reminded him of the painting of the rainbow snake at Uluru, the most recognisable image of all. His sign language was okay, but he found it hard and could only muster the sign for rainbow snake. Surprisingly Balam made the same sign for rainbow snake and said the word "Kulkutan" again. Styles fell still and silent, his head racing trying to understand where this Balam character came from. He asked Balam using sign his answer was "Cholula, Meshikan,

Symbola, Moshe, Yudah, Perusalem Votan".

Like poetry in motion the question was repeated to Styles who gave the reply. "Kalkutun, Astraliyah, Ulurusalem, Tjikurpa" knowing not what else to call it . Styles then told him his name but strangely when Balam repeated this one back to him the word came out as "Stars".

A loud horn blasted and Balam then told Styles using sign, that they would be needed to be seen on deck with all the crew members. He was also warned Styles in the company of others, not to acknowledge him. Balam tried to explain the best he could the pitfalls of them talking in front of the others. As easy as it was for them to converse, Styles did not know if Kalkutun had a word for human, and so he simply called them the Minors. However Balam voiced the word 'Minoors'. They paused then agreed on Moors. Agreeing and needing not explain further they both left and went their separate ways.

Styles left Balam in the living quarters and made his way to the navigation deck above using the spiral staircase to his right. He made his way back up to the deck and was surprised to see a line of men, all stood shoulder to shoulder. They all stood facing Sawyer who had a logbook in hand and was taking a roll call. As Styles shut the door all the men turned to see him. No one said anything and they just watched. Styles looked at Sawyer whether he had seen him or not did not show it, instead, he called out the names from the book only looking up to confirm whoever said the word present.

One by one the men answered and faced Sawyer again. As the names were called and answered, Styles observed the men and tried to remember as best he could all who spoke. "Sailing Master Sawyer" pointing to himself; "Bow' San Stanley" a large strong man with light blonde, grey hair replied 'present". "Carpenter and Surgeon Cofeen" a long-haired Frenchman who smiled at something, from Sawyers world, Styles knew not of.

"Master Gunner Miller" there was no reply, all the men began to look about, Sawyer who did not look up said the name again "MASTER MILLER, I mean Master Gunner Miller". A blonde man with fair skin, who was the only one still looing at Styles, suddenly blinked and turned to face Sawyer then replied present. Sawyer who had now saw that Styles was present closed the book and stopped the role call. "Styles would you be wise enough to report to Senior Almeida." pointing to the Captains cabin." Come and see me later we will talk about your duties". Styles simply nodded and walked passed the line of men who all stared in wonder at the man of darkness. Wearing not much and carrying all of his possessions he strolled passed them looking each one in the eye and wobbling his head as if to acknowledge each one individually.

As he reached for the cabin door at the other side of the deck, the role call continued again. He tapped the door then opened and entered speaking the words "Almeida". Almeida who stood with his back to Styles and had been awaiting his arrival turned as the door closed. "Do you know anything about what we do here Styles?". He didn't really and anything he could of would surely of been the wrong answer. "Not entirely" he replied. "What do you know?" the questions seemed to mock Styles and so he didn't reply straight away. Instead he walked closer to Almeida and stared at the pictures on wall just like Almeida had been. "Pictures like these are important to you", Almeida smiled a little and obviously wanted to hear more. "These pictures are like teachers to you, they tell you things you need to know and must consult them before you do anything". He was right he knew it but Almeida would have a longer broader explanation he thought to himself. "These pictures are what we call maps, they are a detailed drawing of what this world looks like if you were to look at it from the heavens. We use these to make are way about the world without getting lost."

Styles understood but felt entirely lost as to how big or how small the world was. Pointing to the bottom right hand corner of the map, "You see this is where we are Astraliyah, and this is where were going, Madagascar. We will travel across here for about 5 weeks until we reach here." Pointing to the middle of the map. "Let me tell you a story. Where I come from in a place called Europe we see the world full of mystery, the people there do not know what this Earth is about, they don't know much of anything to be honest. Most intelligent does not originate there but is more borrowed copied and stolen from outside of Europe where humanity has long been masters of the arts of architecture, science, magic and the history of the Earth. Europe however could never see past its own nose and waged war on all who oppose her ever since her little less than a thousands years ago." Styles listened and read Almeidas lips. "My ancestor was from the birth place of Europe and was like myself an explorer and Admiral of a large Vessel. His name was Piri Reis and commanded a whole fleet before him. He was a man of many interests and accumulated the largest collection of sea maps known at that time. My ancestor in collaboration with other Europeans decided to make a new revised map of the world using all the source maps he had acquired over his lifetime. After years of craftsmanship and he had finished what would be come to be known as the Piri Reis World Map of 1513. The map had accurately displayed the Southern continents, which were notoriously hard to map given the sheer size. The map depicted the southern coast of South America, Africa and as well a continent further south. For the last 264 years all the different heads of European society have sent out their best navigators to find this southern continent. Until now no one has ever reached this southern continent. This place, which we find ourselves, is not the continent my ancestor wrote about, for it is to small and the 7 mountains present on the map seem to not exist here. My best cartographers tell me that all is correct on the Piri Reis map and that the continent I am looking for is further south still. The legacy of my family since the time of Piri Reis has been to find this lost southern continent. My father only succeeded in dying abroad, his father before him and so on was lost at sea. Now with the advent of the technology I need to travel the world precisely and safely I have managed to navigate here without fault. For the first to find this continent is also the last great explorer of the Earth. That is the legacy of Europe to map the world entirely and I am ashamed to say, dominate". Styles absorbed the information like a plant absorbs sunlight. "Where do I come in to all of this?" There was along pause as Almeida stared at Styles seeing him now as a man ready for whatever he may hear. "Exactly, where do you come in to all this? You are just a man for all intents and purposes an invisible one". Styles remained lost. "Go on " he whispered.

"Where I come from there are those who seek to take all you have. You see no one knows that you all exist here. The lands here are spoken of as uninhabited. No men to speak of, only animals and mineral. It is as though you people hold no claim to this place in the eyes of my people." Almeida had put his point across in the least severe way possible Styles' retorted.

"But we do exist we are the ones who remember the Dreamtime. And when the elders left and the oceans rose we carried the flower of life. When all other men and ceased to be we remained throughout, waiting patiently, learning. Yet you say your greatest minds remain oblivious to our existence."

"That is exactly what I am saying, and you can change all that. We take you back and you can prove what others cannot. I seek to present you to a man who may be the key to achieving this."

Almeida pointed to the map again the one that reminded him of a nine-tailed fox and a hunter. "The man who gave me this map. For the world no longer looks like this."

Almeida needed to focus. "The keys of the past are not all yet revealed to the world. We will do what others have not and will not for their greed exceeds their humanity and I cannot bear it. You see once you see the truth its really quite beautiful and you can learn from it in ways you are still yet to foresee."

Styles who had been listening prominently had deciphered how the world worked according to Almeida and was a little perplexed. How could someone build a ship but not build a relationship. He looked around the room. The tall wooden box that made a ticking noise every second held his attention. "What does this do?"

Looking towards the solemn object pulsing calmly like his heart, Almeida continued to look at Styles for a moment then began to explain the inner working and many uses of a Shelton Regulator. How the Age of the Sail had been hampered almost to the point of normality before the device. It truly was a magnificent device and Almeida almost fell for its charm for a second. "The official story is a man created this device on the promise of payment. Yet he was never paid and further still the device is a recreation of older devices apparently lost to Antiquity. Like almost technology on this Ship it has been recreated from older forms. To the common man of Europe these devices are presented as new amazing discoveries. That is the type of deceit we are dealing with."

A crystal glowed in Styles mind as if it had been rubbed at night and gave off tribo-luminescence." The deceit was beginning to make sense. Plagiarism to the highest degree was rampant he thought. Styles looked towards the large multifaceted crystal tripod on the floor. It reminded him of the finely shaped stones he had found in the sacred wish tree. "It is a little big for you to throw, what is it for." Almeida wondered if that was a reference to the Madagascans or he truly did not know. Either way his training would have to start somewhere and at some point he would come full circle. That pinnacle would be where his training ended he thought. "This is part of the legacy of all the people of the world who lived in the Dreamtime. For by creating the four basic solid shapes and combining them you create this fifth shape, this fifth element.

This shape is actually the shape of the Earth. Imagine for a moment that the Earth is not round but more of a star shape, the seas mud acting as the flesh and fluid of the Earth. "Styles looked bewildered. "Thus a complete Earth would emerge roundish". Styles could feel an attachment to what Almeida was trying to say. Almost as if to help Almeida he pulled out his 5 Neolithic stones he had kept safely stored in his bone bag hanging by his side.

Almeida widened his eyes upon seeing the ancient stones all laced with intersecting lines. He pointed towards the stones and the turned over his hand Styles gave Almeida the brightest of the stones. It was a dodecahedron "You see how the points are placed along intersecting lines. The twelve centres of its pentagonal faces distinguished with further points." The uniform wrapping of these shapes, which were first, made known to us Europeans by Plato naming them after himself of course. Giving him the stone back and taking another one," This one a tetrahedron has four corners that circumscribe into four triangles. They are divided by a further formation of belts determining additional tetrahedrons over the original at midway intervals. These Stones have specific functions and are too intricate for mere hunting purposes especially considering the difference in diet to your people and ours. I have stones similar to these I acquired from France. We used them to create the GaiaStar"

Almeida ran his hands across its surface tracing the hundreds of lines as he spoke. "We melded a Mercator projection world map over the surface and found that this is an excellent tool for distance estimation across the planet. As the sides of the base triangle measure 1400, 2200 and 2600 miles. For example we have found the sides of this base triangle ad dup to 6200 miles, roughly equal to a quarter of the Earths Circumference. It is the perfect object to navigate the sky or Earth with. As you prove still carrying the same stones with you, the stones prove ancient navigators were world wide."

Styles was learning and his brain was working miracles as the moments passed. Then Almeida stated "This is a rhombic tetracontahedron globe." And Styles lost all hope of getting out of this conversation with any type of clarity." Styles on every major surface area of the is globe we find ancient civilisations, everywhere we go." He pointed to different points circling the globe as he went. "Point 44 Astraliyah, we are here, 13 people of the four corners. 1 Complex of Alexandria Cairo. Point 17 the sacred lands of the Hopi. Point 11 the crystal stone circles of the British Isles. And so on."

The captain could assume Styles didn't know half of these places that he spoke of and stopped short. "All of the points across the Earth connect above and underground. Over a third are under control of the new Europeans. The underground rainbow roads are what you see here represented as miniscule lines of reference on the Gaia gift." For one is never lost if one has these two devices." Looking at the Shelton Regulator and the Gaia gift. One is for time and one is for space." Styles understood and finally understood the importance of the Earth Star, the Shelton regulator not so much.

"For yesterday today and tomorrow were all the same if you concentrated hard enough'. He smiled distinguishably. The ocean bound Astraliyahan felt less alien among the navy men. Still smooth precaution followed his every move. There was a rat a tat tat at the door and Styles without hesitation placed the stones back in his bag, as he did one of the stones fell from his grasp just as the hinge of the door squeaked letting in light the smell of salt and Sawyer holding what appeared to be a log book. Styles, who was accustomed to such ways of entering quickly knelt down to pick up the tetrahedron.

A clink was heard close to him that sounded heavy and small. It rolled towards Sawyer and stopped at his thin leather boot. He knelt down to pick it up, but Styles with his long arms and quick wit reached for it first clasping it.

The movement puzzled Senior Almeida. He was not inclined to ask what had startled Styles so much but he felt it better to put his mind at ease. "Thank you Mr Sawyer for the logbook. I expect all in order as far the crew deck and sail?"

"Yes Senior Almeida, all is above board. Shall I proceed to set Sail?" said Sawyer.

"And one more thing. See to it that Styles here taken to the Stock room. Allocate him a portion of the secured stock room, don't rest until Mr Styles' mind is at ease with regards to his affairs."

"Yes Senior Allmeida. Right away Senior Almeida." Sawyer sounded almost ecstatic that he might get to see what Styles held precious to himself. Would there be trinkets that would explain the lightning? Is Styles a danger to the crew?

Without saying anymore, Styles packed up his sapphire disc and stone in to his pouch. They left through the trap door and when they got to the Stock room they heard the hustle and bustle of a full ship crew talking to each other. Some were friends and others were strangers exchanging pleasantries and such. Balam could not be heard, although he had only ever heard him say 2 such things and they both meant so much. Sawyer produced a steel key that unlocked the stockroom door. They entered and closed the door blocking out the noise from the corridor.

There were two port cabin windows filtering light through. On the back wall to the right was a long row of lockers made of metal, they looked solid and fixed to the wall and floor on the front of each was a lock of equal size to the door they had entered. The lockers had bars so that whatever would be stored in side could be seen. He took the design to mean that whatever was stored in them would be too large to just pull out from between the multiple impenetrable arms of the metal prison. In front of him was a large collection of boxes and barrels of varying size. The arrangement rose to his chest. The far left side of the stock room had yet another row of lockers only these ones were not transparent being painted black and larger than the ones on the other side.

Styles wondered which locker would act as his wish tree. A long table behind the door long and low enough to be taken as a seat for where they gravitated.

"Styles within an hour we will set out on a long arduous voyage. It is important to Senior Almeida and all of the crew that you do not do anything stupid and they to you too. For this reason everyone on board must be accounted for and all properties they hold must be registered and stored accordingly. Could you please show me all the object you hold on yourself?"

Without saying anything Styles opened all didgeridoo, pouch and bone bag, he undid the thunderstone from his hair and even produced the acacia seeds, all were laid out on the stock room side table for Sawyer to see. Sawyer looked at all the gems and crystals worth immeasurable amounts in his society. How could such a man have such things he thought to himself? By god a man could buy his own Vessel with riches as this.

Sawyer looked long and hard at the gems that Styles had placed inside of his turtle Shield. Sawyer touched upon the sapphire disk. Moments passed and silently Sawyer picked up the sapphire disk. A sad look came upon his face and he put it back in to the turtle shield. "Is this everything Styles everything that you hold upon on you and all that you hold dear bar your soul?" It was a bit long winded but he understood the question and voiced a "Yes".

"Well then let us see, we have crystals lots of crystals, diamonds, gold, sapphire ring, sapphire disk, a sapphire flower, ah a thunderstone, seeds of some description, a pouch made from some kind of extremely hard metal with what appears to be a three fingered glove? I don't suppose you have safety deposits where you come from?"

Styles didn't get the joke and said nothing. "I just made a wish that's all." Sawyer paused for a moment looking at the rubbing the inside rim of the turtle shield. "Lets not forget the orachleum sword we found you with and the two hand cannons I took back from those dodgies upon the cliff there. Its safe in that locker there." Raising his arm a little in the direction of the middle locker to the left.

"Besides the didgeridoo nothing you have even qualifies as storage, its all either precious gems or and equipment. I didn't expect this I thought they would be these plants here", pointing to the scrunched up handful of acacia flowers, "But this what is it glass" picking up the sapphire bud, Styles watching but remaining silent" The best thing we can do here take you to where you should be. The boss did say to make you comfortable and to be honest if an ABS came across one of these objects he might try and abandon ship. I think it be best if you we give you your personal living space now, rather than later. From what I see you have no weapons to speak of and for some reason have acquired a large amount of vastly expensive stones. The only way to tell for sure how much would be to evaluate the whole collection in Europe. Its safe to say you are not a threat to the crew. The inverse is more like to happen whereby we find you throat cut for just one of your many diamonds."

"Show me to this personal living space then"

Styles watched as Sawyer opened the 4th of 7 lockers revealing a secret door in to an adjacent room. Sawyer turned to Styles with a smile on his face. "What do you know of crystals?". Styles replied quietly " About as much as crystals know of me."

As the sun set in the distance Styles looked directly at the sun for a second. That would have to do. Eyes now closed all was left for the minutes to pass and the ship would further its distance from the shore. His smile slowly returned, it could not have come soon enough. The sound of the ocean lulled him back and forth as he stood there. Easy as it was for him to relax, stood there, a nagging thought in the back of his mind was preventing him from completely relaxing. It wasn't being confined to the quarters or even the thought of the unknown. It was the boomerang shape in the table. He eventually sat down on the soft rug that lay under the nook shelf, just passed the window.

An hour passed by and Sawyer had not returned, the lights were getting low outside and the interior was getting darker. Styles went back to the table that was bare. He took out all the crystals from the pouch pouring them in to a heap. Some of them shone even in the ever-growing darkness. He picked them up one by one rubbing them until each one shone ever so slightly. As if a tiny firebug had trapped itself within each gem. He then took out the sapphire disk. It was larger than all the others and so he rubbed it for a longer amount of time. Soon there was a light burning deep within and he placed it upon the table in the middle. The others he spread in a large circle surrounding the sapphire disk. The more he aligned the direction of the gems so that they arced around the sapphire disk. He took the sapphire ring from his pouch and put it so that it rested on the sapphire disk. Lastly taking the sapphire flower, he placed it on the sapphire ring.

As he did the sapphire arrangement gave off a large glare. It shocked him and his elbow brushed one of the gems close to him, spinning its direction so that it no longer face the other gems, but instead faced the sapphire arrangement. It began to glare up to. Strange as it was, Styles continued to fiddle with axis of each of the gems until he found one that he got the best feeling from. He had made two circles of 16 gems each and placed the flower in the centre of one circle, in the other he placed the flower. The sapphire ring had made its way to his finger and the tightness of it made it difficult fit on. Once on his hand the glow that had beamed within calmed and it with it a drowsiness appeared over him. He felt good and full of energy yet with a mild light headedness.

He held on to the table with both hands and his belly span in circles. It was a strange feeling, almost like the ground was moving below his feet, he knew it was, but this feeling he suspected was more from the ring. He tried to take it off and as the pain swelled in his hand he almost blacked out, with the darkness that he saw something other worldly. It was as if the darkness let him see through the blinding daylight. There under the Ship was something large and alive - something too big to imagine. By the time he had removed the ring he had saw three flashes of something other worldly. He was beginning to regret touching the ring.

As if to reassure himself, though he had to admit, what else could he have done? The damage had been slight and the sapphire had cut his finger bone only slightly. A greasy substance would be needed next time he wore that thing. The ring seemed to hold some kind of power that makes you sea sick and have visions of falling through furniture. He put it back in his pouch.

The light from the flower and sapphire disk were resonating into the surrounding stones. Where some stones had been light a bluish shine appeared form within. Where the stones had looked darker the outside edges now shone with a luminous blue. So the large sapphire stones can charge the other ones, that was good to know he thought and he let out a "huh" although there was no one to here him.

Suddenly a large slam of the what sounded like the storage room door and then the entrance door opened and in walked Sawyer followed by Balam. Seeing Styles avid with crystals Balam closed the door softly and joined Styles and Sawyer by the table. They all nodded to each other then reverted their eyes back to the table. "Balam tells me you two have already been acquainted and that you have more than skin colour in common". He looked at Balam remembering their conversation to not mention their knowing of each other. What kind of game was Balam trying to pull here?

Sawyer couldn't of been happier at the fact it seemed. So Styles just went along with the show, "Yes Kalkatan Kulkatan." Balam obviously wasn't prepared for that one. "What" Sawyer asked. "It's just a greeting we make when we met each other." "Okay, katungya that a native thing?" Styles wasn't sure if that was a jibe or a compliment. "Something like that, yeah something like that" as he looked back at the Balam. Sawyer looked around the room to see if Styles had been up to much, he walked around the room checking the cloth on the pyramid shape before returning. "Styles, let me break news to you, you are going to be with us for a while whether you like it or not, whether I like you or not, or whether you like us or not. It really is all just potatoes. "

Styles looked confused and defensive. Balam also but kept his cool, it was hardly a charming introduction to social etiquette, among a situation as being confined to a ship for more than 2 months at a time? Sawyer looked down at the table and saw the sapphire disk underneath the flower. He stroked the leaf of the flower then brushed it a side form the disk picking it up and admiring it close up. Styles could now see from Sawyers expression that he remembered the disk from earlier on in Senior Almeidas quarters.

Now, here he was an hour later with it in his grasp. He had no reason not to trust him, other than he had his own prejudices towards the humans. After all the man had offered to help him store his precious items. How bad a man could he be really? Then the thought of Sawyer killing all those people, as brutal as it was, it had been to protect him. For what an Astraliyahan boy who even Styles knew next to little amount.

"Il tell you some true words, listen good because I wont repeat them. I come to your land with my men in tow, a ship with weapons and men and intentions that must be carried out. We travelled for many months to arrive on your shores hungry and tired, dried from the sea and washed again, day in day and out for months. We have taken no treasure, no gold, no women to speak of; all we have is you and your god given gift of speech. A mad mission if I ever knew one oh and do I know one. You see Mr Balam here, he comes from a land as far from me as it is to you, a land we passed to come here. A land we shall never return to. My people first came to Balams land some 300 years ago. A Father Benito went to the Mixtec capital of Achiotlan. There stands a pyramid covered in volcanic ash that erupted and brought fire down on the people many thousands of years ago. This father Benitio was presented with an Emerald the size of a pepper pod. The craftsmanship of the engraving is unmatched to this day. Father Bentito had the Emerald powdered, mixed with water and poured to the Earth, he then dug his boots over the ground. Funny here we are few hundred years later and I see Senior Almeida and you together with the sapphire, makes me appreciate the shit we've got, I mean it could always be worse. Instead you're in top class company riding the oceans with one of the best crews I've ever heard of, you kent beat that".

Balam was looking down at the floor obviously remembering the pain of what his people were going through even now. There was an air of tension rising from within the room. The vibe coming from Balam looked like he wanted to hurt someone, as if he was relieving a horrific scene from his ancestor's days in Mexico. Why was Balam projecting these feelings onto Sawyer? What could Sawyer have possibly done wrong? There wasn't any obvious crime or reason. Balam looked towards him with eyes of someone vexed, yet truthful. That's all Styles could get from it. He didn't pick up any readings from Balam and so he resigned to forget about it. Sawyer who was definitely feeling the vibes in the air spoke no more of the ill fated or the Emerald of the mixtec Capital Achiotlan.

Sawyer wanted to change the subject on to things more pressing. Balam ceased to talk and wandered of slowly towards the books on the shelves. A moment of sheer trivialness swayed Balam back in to fray speaking to the wall yet loud enough for all in the room to hear." Scrolls, thousands upon thousands of scrolls, telling of my peoples past were took by the Europeans. In the main square of Mani, just south of the Merrida Yucutan province, countless statues of gold and silver outlining our histories past were all melted down and taken by these Europeans. The truth of all men's past, burnt away in these documents and so called "idols". It was calculated so that we had no chance. Only 20 of such codices remain, here guarded under lock and key." Sawyer who had no choice but listen waited for Balam to continue.

Styles listened, this was troubling Balam greatly. "Styles those who fail to learn from the past are doomed to repeat it. There was a man back then a man called Juan de Zumarraga he burnt over 20,000 statues that represented our people through lifetime to lifetime. Over 500 temples we had erected above the ancient ones creations. The monuments of stone we had settled to live on top of using the tunnels and undergrounds peacefully. For 11 years this man commanded his people to steal all our astronomical documents. Then they burnt it all in the main square of Mani. Our people mourned immensely and the ties of hatred attached itself to our lands."

Balam was looking at Sawyer directly. Styles looked at Sawyer who was looked at him and then to the wall, "Well this is not helping, dragging up the past I mean, your going on as if I was the one who did it". The both looked at Sawyer for a moment, as he got all defensive. Styles could see what he meant by the remark and said " I know what you mean, just because your European, it doesn't make you one of them."

"I am going to get some fresh air. Styles it was good to talk to you, Balam come let us all leave this place I'm sure Styles will want some peace and quiet". Sawyer produced a second key from his pocket. "Here Styles take this key. It will get you in and out of both storage rooms, please remember to keep all your most treasure valuables here because god forbid we capsized. Here is a key for one of the lockers in the storage room. In it you will find clothes and food I suggest you put them on when above deck."

He took the second key from him and waited for them both to leave before clearing his throat and arranging all his affairs. He untwisted his didgeridoo and placed all the crystals in side. Clicking the hidden compartment back in to place, he felt safer aboard the Vessel. He went in to the next room and got changed in to clothes that had been laid out for him. There was a pair of long johns and rubber boots the likes of which he was unaccustomed to. He did like how he could feel the ground beneath his feet and removed them again. The rest was a white cotton cord neck shirt with trouser made of hemp - very uncomfortable. He wasn't going to wear any of it.

He left the room and went to find Senior Almeida, taking the lower deck entrance to his quarters. The sounds of the instruments were no more to be heard. Not wanting to stop, he went directly through the rooms, up the spiral stairway and nocked the trap door. There was no answer and so he entered. Kerosene lamps lighted the room. Almeida sat solemn on a chair staring at the map on the wall. From that angle, Styles could see that Senior Almeida was fidgeting with something in his hands, but he couldn't see what. The door closed and Almeida turned around he to see Styles. "Styles I want to tell you something you should know, these words were told to me by Pinpin. He and your mother wanted to tell you themselves one day. I guess they hoped it would never fall on you they way it has. You have even had to kill a man.

Styles laughed at the man. It was not that he found killing a laughing matter, it was more that he knew that the man was not dead as Senior Almeida had so dramatically put it. Almeida continued more cautiously with his words as if he had taken the laugh to be manic. He pointed to the map showing "The vast different Goddoms, Queendoms and Kingdoms of the ancient world." The diamond areas that uniformly and gracefully skeletonized the map. There was no area on the map that did not fit in the intricately fit diamond row across the centre of the map.

Almeida scratched his beard slowly pulling fluff from his chin. "Those tunnels encompass the whole globe. These diamond marks on the map show where the entrances are." The power that surrounds all of these points is immense and free. The giant structures of the planet made of Stone were all able to communicate with each other, information and energy was transferred freely all across the globe. Each location on the Earth, and there are many, would act as receiver or senders for all types information energy and life. When the flood came the waters around the planet rose more than 400 feet, leaving not many places to hide. It was a worldwide event and there was nowhere unaffected. A lot of life on the planet drowned or adapted.

You know the only original place that was left was Astraliyah. The only place that wasn't flooded I mean. Imagine the whole world drowning, every Kingdom, Queendom and Goddom." He pointed to the hunter and lizard painting. "This is Earth before the waters and this" pointing to the painting to his left of the hunters head and other weirdly shaped things. "Is the world as we know it now. A lot less land mass as you see. There were only a handful of holy places that managed to continue their schools of knowledge and wisdom. Chiefly your people of Astraliyah who apart from surviving the Ice age unaffected have full control of their rainbow road."

Styles found it fascinating to hear this from a minor. Carry on human he thought. There is only so many lies you can tell until you stand in your own mess. He liked Senior Almeida but wasn't sure why a human would want to talk about the ways before they existed. "So tell me so Almeida, what do I, Styles, need to know?" Almeida knew his slow speech infuriated the Astraliyahan. "The flood, it kept a lot of places hidden, for over 17,000 years of miracles of stone too large to be handled by muscle stood silent across the world. People, Earth multiplying and worshipping what they know not. Some of the original men who survived the flood sought out the old power systems made of stone. With their teachings again they set man on a safer path. The canals of Europe were cold desolate areas. Your Tribe the Ananangu are like many others who I have paved new ground to find. All of these tribes have gatekeepers like your father. Who generation to generation protect the gates from and keep order. Where the world was just too barren after the flood the gates were never again protected.

Thousands of seasons changed and snow and fire and mountain replaced technology. This place is now known as Europe and the new masters have found all of their energy centres. They build cities around them and seek to conquest wherever the rainbow roads lead. In the Americas, the Europeans have taken the tunnels. All the underground tunnels are connected. Some are damaged but eventually they will come for Australia too.- by land and underground. They have even designed something called a train, which can travel through these tunnels using the same metal strip we use to transport us without damaging the mag force. These trains are wide and using them leaves no room for anyone else in the tunnels. Very dangerous for people - like Pinpin. I fear Pinpin has left for the Goddom of the far south. If only to warn the people there of the impending arrival of the humans. I imagine he has contacted the people of the south to warn them or he was banished by your people, as I know sometime sthe dreaming can do."

It all made sense to him. His father knowing some secret people of the south, coincidently Almeida's family had been searching for this same place for generations now and here at the end of it all, was Styles and the crew of the Vessel.

"Now Styles, for solidarity of companies sake, I will issue a memo to all the crew that you have not yet experienced the smallpox and with that said you should be confined to the storage area throughout the sleeping part of this journey. This will give you time to study.

MAURITIUS MAHEBORG

1778. The day that word had come of arrival was a busy one, All hands were on deck. A small boat was hoisted down from the middle of the starboard and a large hold all backpack was placed in side as well as a hand cannon. It was a very small supply to take for everyone. It wasn't until two sailors with rifles followed by Sawyer arrived, that the boat was hoisted to the waters below.

Words were exchanged with Senior Almeida and then Sawyer shook Almeida's hand. All saluted Sawyer and then he went over board with the sailors. With four oars, they rowed to the island on the right. It was the first bit of inhabited land that they had seen in over three weeks.

Balam later explained to Styles, that Sawyer and the sailors had gone to Rodrigues Island. Nothing more was said of then and the crew leaving. Senior Almeida watched with Stan the Boatswain, until the men had made it to shore. The anchor was raised and onwards the Vessel headed west. Styles had not spoken to Senior Almeida since that night with Balam in the living quarters. He didn't think Senior Almeida was ignoring him, it was a more that he seemed to be ignoring everyone.

That evening he went to see Balam and soon they were talking deeply about all things that passed their calm minds. Soon they faced the subject of Sawyer and the sailors. Balam told him "Sawyer was to go to a cave on the island that leads to a cave in Mauritius. Senior Almeida was positive the shallows of Rodriguez in the caves had subsided enough to descend in to the rainbow circuit. The road leads east to Astraliyah and west to Mauritius. Rodriguez was an ancient temple of sorts on top perched on the summit of and underwater city. Numerous caves and labyrinths of coral limestone to attend with and he would find his way to Mauritius- or not! They would then rendezvous on southern most point of Mauritius where long there had been an exit from the rainbow road of Rodriguez. Recon."

As they sat there with the shrine painting of the ancient Olmec head, the Aztec explained that "Senior Almeida has in his possession the Smoking Mirror Of Tezcatlipoca. With it he see's the whole cosmos." Styles still didn't understand how the cosmos could guide someone on Earth unless of course for navigation. Balam explained further "The smoking mirror is the Earth with all of its monuments, mountains, rivers and valleys, they are all positioned to mirror the sky and all that lays within it. Almeida can use the sky map and Earthstar to find any sacred ground he needs to. He is not part of the Ancients or the European humans although he is human; his ends are his own crafted from a family legacy. Father to son, father to son, when he dies, his son automatically takes over. There life on Malta is Truman show where they are destined to search for Antarctica. Yet they have no sure way of ever getting there, Soon you will see if you have not already".

Two days later while travelling on the warm west winds the Vessel slowed its creep toward the south east coast of Mauritius. A French traders flag was raised at full mast to signal and all signs Astraliyah were stored in the storage room. Styles had left all items there, apart from his thunderstone and 2 diamonds, which he kept in his pouch. The door was locked and the key was placed in Almeida's safe living quarters in a bowl of fruit. As Almeida returned on deck, he saw the panoramic of Mauritius for the first time.

Like Rodriguez, the island lay solemn in a never-ending

blue bed. The protruding mountains from the otherwise flat landscape, spined the Island. The whole left of the island was flat and green and was a perfect seat for the master of the island. The mountain in front of him defied the belief of the humans. Seated Like a cat floating on a raft, the giant panthera of stone dwarfed the ridiculously named Grand Port below.

The humans were oblivious to the ancient workings of the planet. Disguised as a mountain, gazing eastwards towards the ocean and the waters below. Styles wondered how long the lion had been watching and waiting for his arrival. How much longer it would wait. Tall black ebony trees grew up to the side of the mountain. It lay on the right hand side of a large Bay. Styles went to front of the ship to see the lion mountain better. He drew in a large breath as if preparing for underwater submersion and closed his eyes. He focused only on the cool blowing breeze behind his ears. He called out to the lion and gave thanks that it still stood gazing. He remembered Uluru floating and opened his eyes again absorbing every curve of the colossal Sphinx.

Stan the boatswain came over eating what he thought to be dried salted fish. He had still not eaten, yet the constant temptation of sweet smelling foods led him to question the mortality of humans. Senior Almeida having previously pulled Styles, Sawyer and Balam into his cabin explaining the need to find an entrance in to the underground. A map on the wall of his cabin showed Mauritius and points of interest. "Over a hundred cave entrances and I expect one atoll lead us to the underground." The rainbow road on the map going straight to Madagascar, underneath an ocean of water. Thoughts of flooded tunnels or worse, large creations of metal squeezing through the tunnels at unstoppable speeds. He wished the tunnels were flooded and then the humans would have to wait, maybe even change their approach to the accessing the rainbow road. He would remain hopeful.

Senior Almeida was present for a role call on deck before docking. A team headed by Stan would leave for supplies and repairs of the Ship. While another headed by Senior Almeida would go a land with Styles, Balam and Sawyer, to further the 'expedition'. They would all regroup on the other side of the island. Having no bounties or warrants and under the guise of a slave ship the Vessel docked in port. The Grand Port Senior Almeida presented his papers, which were all in order.

When they left the ship as a group of twelve they felt safe - as a group. The port was sunny and bustling, the smell of sea air and Ylang Ylang encroached on the group of eight. Stan and the 3 sailors had rifles harnessed on their back. All dressed in blue military colours they walked ahead of Almeida's team. The dock was long and wooden. A box lay at the exit of the yard. The large moustached man guards dressed in blue were presented with a document stamped in France for the acquisition and transport of two persons of black colour. These persons are to be left unmolested as they are to be transported back to France. This was signed "Charles de Epee, Paris France." The smaller of the two guards in the box stood up and walked to wards Balam who was dressed in his flowing red robe looking at it with envy.

"Cette robe, tu est une arab?", Senior Almeida who spoke French replied "No monsieur ce une tribal vetement, sacred mait pas religious. The guard who listened hard and found the accent of Senior Almeida to be correct attacked "Il ne pas de sacred sans du religion". "Il ne busain baptism," looking at Styles he carried on "Le deux en faite". "Vien direct a ala eglise de Mahebourg, tout suite!". The guard pointed back towards the dock towards the other side of the dock. Smoke could be seen past trees. There was a large boat at the end of the dock that could take them to Mahebourg.

Balam who was looking more nervous by the second, began to look at the floor. Senior Almeida then paid the two guards with a small purse of French coins. The larger of the guards took the purse and thanked Senior Almeida. The smaller of the two who had not seen how much was inside, couldn't help himself and shouted in English so that the others understood. "Your slaves must be baptised today, they will be inquiries made tomorrow morning at le eglise de mahebourg. Oublier pas!" The group had no choice but to listen but continued slowly in to the Grand Porte.

There were many different types of people walking around in bay. A row of stone houses had been erected below the mountainside. A large mast from a ship stood at the end of the houses with a French flag at topmast, flapping in the breeze. The trees behind the houses and mountainside shook with the warm breeze. The smell of vegetation filled the nostrils of the sea wary lot. There would be no deviations from their goals in front of Senior Almeida. It was obvious one of the sailors wanted to buy some sweet bread from the last house that looked a little dirtier than the rest. Stan pulled the man by the shoulder, then looking, he nudged his way towards the front of the group. Behind the houses two guards dressed in blue stood against the wall, they were talking amongst themselves, until one of them caught the eye of Styles.

The man got off the wall and gave Styles a mean stare. Styles couldn't understand why the human was angry with him. Half a kilometre later the man was far from view, the pathway split at a junction, turning left so that they might go through the baptism. The group crossed a small river by is shallowest point. Continuing to walk southwards for just over and hour, they arrived at the coastal Village. The conditions were of which were applauding.

There was a large square outside of a large churchyard. Within the churchyard was a slave market. Men, woman and children went back and forth across the market all day, bought and sold. The slaves wore no clothes of value and so when Balam entered the square, all eyes immediately turned on him. Five local Europeans who were accustomed to barbarity came over to Balam pulling at his robe. Balam was quickly becoming the centre of attention with his flowing red cape. Soon, a man from the group of Barbarians, talking French and with seriousness said, "Who ya master, whos ya master."

Stanley stepped in front of him. "This man needs to be christened. The two of them." Shouting towards Styles. A missionary man appeared from among the slave traders." Are you the owner of said Slaves". Almeida looked at Styles and Balam cringing with the thought of what he was about to say "These men are crew aboard my Ship. Your laws here say they must be baptised if I am to use them here". The preacher man looked at Balams robes once more " And just what do you do with these slaves?" Almeida not taking any more time then he needed to said "A mans business is his own... say that to others as dark nights fall upon mothers of this land." Stan set off almost without saying a word in the direction of the food market taking the armed sailors with him.

The preacher who saw the weapons of the troop as people not to be trifled with, Balam had not said a word with his mouth yet his towering stance and firm hand under his cloak said so much more. "je mappele Francois, ce une eglise du deux, deux baptisme au jourdhi, ce ne pas possible" A silver piece later and Styles was in the midst of a simple baptism. He was looking around the garden of the church admiring the flowers when he was asked to say "amen". Water was poured on his head and he was given a piece of sweet bread as penance, which he put in his mouth and did not swallow. He stepped back and tried to blend in as much as he could.

The second baptism was not as simple. Balam was asked to remove his robe by the priest and only after approval from Senior Almeida did he do so. Balam faced the priest repeated words when asked. The crew tried to hide their amazement at what they saw on the Toltecs's back. Under both shoulder blades he had two emeralds the size of hazelnuts. Styles spat the bread in to his hand and hid it in his hand. Holding it tightly so that peering eyes may see. As the priest came to the end of the ceremony, he lowered Balam with a hand on his shoulder in to a seated position. Reaching for the cup on the precipice he proceeded to pour the salted water on to his head and back. The catholic fanatic stopped talking to take a closer look at the dark skinned man.

On either side of Balams back were crystals the size of hazelnuts. The priest was startled by the way the skin had grown around the gems. He then walked away and returned quickly with a member of the government who had been stood in the courtyard. The next word said to Almeida was that "No baptism can take place" and the man would be "Sent to hell" unless the gems were removed. The loud slanders made by the priest attracted a congregation of locals from the slave market. Almeida and Sawyer unable to do anything as a wild group of citizens demanded the crystals be removed from Balams back.

He remained silent knowing his situation could worsen; this was a test at best. Senior Almeida argued the best he could in defence of Balam keeping them. Even Sawyer made large threats until another official from the government who was dining in the area came along. It was decided that Stanley should remove the gems with a scalpel, which arrived with no anaesthetic. Balam was offered no alcohol and remained silent. The jealous preacher had the gems removed from his back one by one waiting in patiently with his skinny wristed hands held out waiting to clean the blood off the ancient orbs with his holy cloth. He paid no attention to the obvious torment the Toltec had just gone through

Stan said a few kind words. Styles looked at the sailors who kept congregators from peering in to the apparent madness, which had best the church. After the two were remove, the descendant of the jaguar people let out a large cry. At first just a cry but then it turned in to a word "ACAB". The priest then disappeared with the government official for moment, leaving Balam to put back on his robe. He was not stitched up and left in a very bad condition. Balam took it all in his stride and he just sat there. As if he would never be surprised as to what nightmares could befall a person.

When the priest and official returned they said that a baptism would go ahead. Senior Almeida told the priest to keep the gems they had acquired. Leaving out the back door and through across the cemetery the crew of four eventually arrived back on the road toward Grand Port Bay. As they descended the hill, Styles contemplated the way of the human. He looked at the back of Senior Almeida as he led them down the hill, Balam then Styles and Stanley.

Almeida stopped for a moment. He took out a small map and compass. Balam was transfixed on the ocean staring away his pain. Stanley was staring at the Balam. "I'm really sorry man that I had to do that" He was going to say something, then Almeida said "That Lion mountain in the distance is maybe seven kilometres". Stanley stopped talking, which eased Balam's pain.

Quite frankly he had accepted what had happened to him. He began to pick up mud from the ground and rub it in to his wounds. Almeida kept talking about the lion mountain, the cat mountain that looked out to Styles' home, thousands of kilometres away. Almeida was divulging more of how much he knew. It kept their minds of past events and he had to hand it to him. It had changed the mood. The men got up and walked on. Stanley went back to the church to take the soldiers and supplies back to the ship. He had given the wounded some time to escape the blood thirsty Christians.

The long wide bay glistened in the blistering heat. A line of trees running on top of the hillside was a perfect shade for the human. Only the cool breeze that flew from the west, sometimes swirling the long grass and rocking the cane back and forth, faced this heat they had found themselves in. Walking together Styles could not shake the feeling of loss. Here he was walking again only without the can man Nipnip. Although he knew his old friend could not live outside of Uluru he missed the walks they had taken together those last seven years.

The birds tweeted all around and soon they were in the shades of the black ebony trees. The monstrous trees provided ample shade of the group. Styles saw a large pink pigeon to the left. No sooner had he pointed towards the unfortunate bird it had flown away. The chime of the church bell rang twice and a large choir of birds sang a song as lovely as the wood was. A couple of girls voices and a French mans was heard followed by a shot from a large rifle. It was for enough away for the team of three to not change course.

Maybe a woman needed help Styles thought, but Almeida turned to him and put his finger to his mouth signalling to be quiet. With that they marched a mile through the wood. The path was beaten and the ground looked to be of stone. The trees had grown on top of the ground, but Styles could see the perfectly flat ground and seams trawling off as high slopes were climbed. The rock was enormous and continued in formed blocks all around them. The trees birds, wildlife had all come afterwards. These 'roads' had been erected long before any human had been there. The handiwork of the Madagascans of long ago he thought to himself.

The diversity of life in the forest begged belief and it

was as if some guiding hand had left the seeds of life to grow. As the forest ended, the ground became sloped and natural once more. The descended through another sugar cane field, although this one had recently been harvested. The yield couldn't have been of consequence because large chevron lay here and there fallen from a storm, underneath a small patch of cane still grew through the semi dry branches of the broken tree. The rushing of water and the smell of sea salt once again filled his nostrils. For some reason the feeling brought him warm emotions and he realised he felt safer on the vessel than he did here in Mauritius.

They arrived at the river des Creoles and followed the embankment leftwards until they came to a large log that had been felled. It was dry and they crossed one by one. Styles crossed first and looking down noticed a school of Goby fish swimming up stream inland. The land rose to a lush green forest and swerving right they arrived at a path that run parallel to the edge it. To the right were terraces and the slaves were seen therein, farming at gunpoint. The ever growing suspicion that something was terribly wrong with the world tried to reach in to Styles's mind. As the terraces altered their path they were forced to descend, following a long road of dirt. Either side men and women worked hard in the blistering heat. The French soldiers and merchants together factorised a nation. The only reason Styles could see for their absolute submissiveness was the violent manner in which the human's treated the natives. The dreadful echo of torment was all around him.

Balam had again returned to his cold stare. He was aiming his hostility out towards the humans, uttering menaces and protective words under his breath. Senior Almeida guided them through and after a while the bodies all around were only behind - only a memory. The end of the fields brought them back on the main road, which lead back to the Grand Port.

The three of them arriving at the by footpath at the Grand Port all looked disheartened to see the same two soldiers leaning against the side wall of a house, as if their whole purpose in life was to test things, test walls and test people. The first one to make eye contact was the one on the right, The other was staring at some local dark skinned women, who were busy making a fire, burning all the litter that would otherwise scatter across the land bringing disease.

It was about afternoon time and the smoke smelled nice coupled with the Mauritian air. The soldier nudged his colleague as if to say stand at attention, but the manner in which he acted afterwards presented a more sinister motive. They were both now making eye contact with Balam. This infuriated the soldiers and Almeida had to walk in front of Balam just to cut the visual jousting. He then turned his direction completely to the left taking the fork in the road, which lead to the lion mountain. The soldiers never came closer than 30 metres. It still felt very close as Styles felt the eyes of the human all over him.

The woman who was making the fire, did not look up. The rag clothes she had, could not of darkened her light. Her face was a kind of beauty Styles had not seen before. As he got closer to her ,he saw large slices down her back. The cloth she wore as a kind of jumper skirt was very loose fitting and it seemed to be very uncomfortable. He wanted to hold out his hand and touch her and he almost did as he watched her, getting closer all the while. Her hair was short and her eyes were very light, her skin as dark as his on a cold day.

As he walked past, she bravely continued her burning. Three dark men were working tirelessly digging at the ground with pick axes. Another human with no soldier uniform watched them. He was sat on a wicker chair in the shade of a takamaka palm, drinking from a bottle. The wind blew from the Grand Port blowing smoke across the path through Styles and co, into the shade of the palm. The man peered at them from through the smoke and stood up to get away from the smoke. Once the smoke blew past the palm the man looked at over at them just as they were passing the corner of a large rock. The temperature dropped slightly in the shade of it and continued with the trees line towards the summit of the mountain.

A kilometre later, they took a left and went up a steep path round the side of the feline shaped limestone. As they got higher up through the canopy of trees the sound of wildlife surround them. The mountain could have told him so much, he thought, if only he had brought his teachers with him. The hissing of a Boa universal to anyone but a human, that all would be right with the world, prompted Balam to ask "Senior Almeida, Where do we go?"

"Defeating the path of this mountain will lead to the answer you seek." The pace continued and Styles took the lead. Two hundred metres up and the path turned right, climbing steeper. After handfuls of trouble climbing the lizard infested clumps mountainside they arrived 30 metres higher on the summit of Lion Mountain. Almeida, the last one to finish cleaning himself from the dirt on his shoulders, pulled out a map and compass. After staring at the scroll of paper and turning so that he faced north. He whispered to himself. Styles becoming more interested, Balam not so much. Then turned on his heels 45° so that he was facing the interior of the forest and the heart of the island. Styles and Balam looked at mountain opposite them.

"We must meet Sawyer in this direction. We can make it by nightfall and wait for Stanley's arrival". A day gecko as big as the flower it ran by stopped in front of Styles. The three of them looked at it. Styles moved his foot and it ran off across the back of Lion Mountain. Almeida turned towards the Vieux Grand Port below. "The Vessel is on route to Port Loui as I speak. We shall make our way to the rendezvous with Sawyer." He didn't say anymore than that he just set off towards the mountain in the distance.

There were no trees at the base of the mountain. A mile wide stretch of cane fields leads them to the next mountain. Twenty 20 minutes of nothing but cane and Myrna birds, when Styles saw the first ox drawn cart that had made the path they were walking along. An Indian man with a guarded look on his swollen brow, guided the ox slowly to a halt and began to load up the cart with tools. Large sacks filled with stones rolled when he threw them on the cart.

The man said nothing as they passed. The cane fields lowered to mud and they crossed another stream through a shallow point that moistened their feet. As they again saw wildlife, the three shared a happy moment in the shade of the many ebony trees that always appeared at the right moments, as if the land had been created with thoughts as these in mind. A Rosa deer drank up river and had not been tempered enough to leave. Cumbersome goby fish tickled the feet of Stylyes and Balam, who both walked barefoot.

After crossing, they all climbed the steep red soil embankment. Styles noticed the boa snake in the river. It was a metre long, even winding and fat. It looked happy just cruising along. The goby fish did not change direction either. As they climbed out of the embankment they spoke not a word, but shared an invisible smile. Senior Almeidas shoes were wet and squelched as he walked. The three of them walked over and up the grassy ground. For miles on either side the cane fields locusts and Myrna birds sang songs of pain. The wind blew in their ears as if the orchestra required the wind to master the sega hymn. Once they were at the highest most point between Lion Mountain and Creole Mountain they came across two pyramids 12 metres tall.

The ground all around them was flat. Styles did what he did naturally. He climbed the pyramid to see what there was to see. Balam and Almeida stood and watched, whether too tired or wounded to even try they continued on. Styles looked at them. Beyond the pyramids, midst's of cane fields, he could see another five. The buildings could only be as old the cane fields, he thought to himself. The cane fields the humans had cropped grew over more and more land. The sky crackled with thunder and Styles wondered if the Earth would die screaming.

The fields of cane were all around him, near and far. A scheme to take these Creole people, forcing them to farm cane for them. Whipped beaten, shot, were the obvious reasons why these people would continue.

Like scattered promises Styles knew he couldn't help them by using his fists. The technology the oppressors used were the only device that stopped these people fighting back. He climbed down and caught up to Balam and Almeida. It was clear to him they had encountered the pyramids before because of the disregard they held for these monuments. Something was going down. He had to admit they it all intrigued him. As he walked, he counted - Seven of them. All made of rock with no mortar or cement to fix them together. He arched his neck up at the sky, looking for the seven and laughed realising his genius and also the fact the sun hadn't yet set. The sun was setting directly behind Lion Mountain from his viewpoint in the middle of the seven creations of stone.

Hours would pass before he would be able to compare them to the Seven Sisters of the night sky. By then he would have been far-gone. He also wondered how the lion know which direction the sun would set if he was not real? The ground between the pyramids was not used directly for slave labour; it was if this specific was sacred event to the humans. Used by the humans for fear or understanding, he was not yet sure. He felt stronger knowing the lion stone stood unmoved. As he looked to the people he began to sweat. For a moment he saw the enslaved workers looking beyond him. He turned around to see the "halo'd Lion". Luminous light hovered over the mountain for all to see.

The blue of the ocean had transfixed almost everyone. The mountain went a shade of red and shone as if gold was the true make up of the monument from before vision or word could impede on that moment. As the light went further from view they turned and continued there walk through the slave fields. Balam and Styles protected by a human called Almeida. As if tiny prayers had been answers, the locusts continued to eat the canes that were worked by the blighted men and women of Mauritius. Every now and again the perverse laugh of the Myrna was heard as they chose their locust carefully and then ate them.

MAURITIUS MAHEBOURG

It was nighttime night when they arrived at the base of Creole mountain. They had been on the island 12 hours. They made camp at the base of the mountain. Almeida checked his map and compass to make sure nothing was amiss. Styles made a fire and Balam helped him by collecting twigs, brush and fire wood. As they settled down on beds of leaves they stared in to the flame, burning under a moonless sky. Almeida went to sleep more or less straight away, the other two sat there talking in sign language.

Styles asked Balam how he had dealt with the painful extraction of gems and the unholy Balam replied simply that the only way to get through such an ordeal would be to remember what he was here for. That the end goal was more important than the pain the missionaries had ordered. Balam explained that the land he came from had been under occupation by humans for over three hundred years. They called it "1492". There were few places in Balams land where the "conquistadores/conquerors" and Spanish had not yet vandalised. The physical underground networks his people were guardians of were falling one by one to the humans.

He was sold in to slavery to Senior Almeida. He soon found out that Almeida was not like most slave masters. He had never asked him to do anything that would normally be required of a slave. Almeida simply required knowledge and information. He was asked to write and draw as much as he could of his people and the people who had been in the lands before his. The monuments of the people of his land and civilisation, Columbus and Polo came upon when they first came to the Old Mechican Lands. Most other Europeans aboard considered Balams way of reconnecting to the past to be blasphemous as the main religion of them was Christianity. Almeida admitted that he knew the history of American man was far more advanced then the Papal Bull doctrine would allow.

Styles wanted to know more of Balams religion and this thing called Christianity, but Balam begged him to save those questions for when they were safely re-aboard the Vessel. Balam would not admit, but it was as though he feared punishment of his beliefs. Styles could hardly blame him they had been duped in to a baptism of the human's religion only to be coerced in to a barbaric surgical procedure.

They lay down to sleep for the night. Styles realised as he lay there that he lay there that people outside of his domain were not as prepared for this life. They needed to sleep more than he ever did. He wondered if Balam had always this tired? And how many of his people still lived and retained the source of knowledge of all that was in America and the world, only three hundred years earlier. As Balam lay there with his back to Styles, he lay there sleepless without his normal routine of Astraliyah. He wondered if Balam could dream of the past like Pinpin.

Closing his eyes just like Balam. Within a few moments he had fallen in to a deep sleep. The next moment he opened his eye, the sky was bright once again. At first he had problems remembering where he was. The trees were different to Astraliyah and he sat up in shock as soon as his second eye had opened.

His first night on Mauritius had been calm and uneventful; he hoped the next day would bring the same. Although he had mentally prepared himself for what lay ahead, he knew the muddy point of view here and it was disgusted him. How could people treat each other this way, he thought to himself.

Almeida ate some dried fish from his leather satchel. Taking a bottle from his side he drank sparingly. Never once offering Balam or Styles. Did he know that the two did not have to eat food as he did? It was looking so. For Styles at least had never ate so much as a leaf since arriving with the humans. His belly rumbled for the first time since he could remember. Almeida looked to Styles and offered him some dry fish. Styles didn't answer but the look on his face maybe did. "Do you want a piece?" Styles had never eaten a fish and did not intend to do so now "I am enough" was all he said. Balam, who took out from his cloak some dried fruits and ate them slowly. Almeida offered the bottle and they both said no. The bottle smelt faintly of pungent wine and the stench of alcohol was no good for anyone, Styles thought to himself.

After he watched the two eat their breakfast he went for a walk on his own. He found a tree and took a small folded leaf of the white gold powder from within his hair. The thumbnail sized leaf contained a few dried droplets of golden powder. He brought it to his noise and sniffed it all in. As soon as he had he held his breathing it on himself. The actions of a man who was not ready to give away his secrets away, not yet anyway.. The powder was gone and he ate the leaf. He was in strange lands and so he took no chances. The gold on the other hand tasted like gold. Without the metallic taste, zero magnetism for added flavour he thought to himself.

Black and yellow wasps buzzed out from behind a savannah palm gaining the attention of Styles. All golden. At first two appeared and then deciding against an all out show. He said "Uluwah" and one of them circled a few times then went back in to the bush. The black and yellow neighbour camouflaged occasionally by the boucle d'oreille's that grew nearby. Returning he saw Almeida taking a comical piss in to the bushes. Balam had leaves in his hand. Spiking them with thorns. After shaking his hips Almeida returned. Relieved of the fumes in his lungs. He was sweating and admitted he had "Ate too much fish". By his reckoning the sun had risen around 5.45.

Loud birds shrieked all morning, calling their fellow fouls. Almeida then laid out the plans for the day. Heading east along the base of the Creole mountain range, towards the centre of the Island they would rendezvous with Sawyer. Back to Port Louis a couple of miles further north.

They packed up and set off further down the path that had brought them so far. The warm morning was particular dry. The birds tweeted and the trees danced. The wind blew a dry breeze over the tops of trees. About 4 kilometres later, a large square summit could be seen. Almeida again took out his map and compass pointing to various squiggles and then to the summit. "That summit over there is Le Pouce, the highest mountain here! To the East, that large Chiant stood on top of that mountain there is Pieter Both! Can you see it?"

Styles looked a good 15KM to the right and saw the monuments where humanoid like figure stood. The mountain had been sculpted to resemble a human, a Stone face Monument reaching in the sky and the past of Mauritius. Standing 800 metres tall. "That is where we will meet Sawyer.

As they walked ever closer to their destination, the sun got higher in the sky and as the light came with it Styles felt completely revitalized. The gold was obviously doing something good for him. Balam, who was also an extremely able bodied individual, managed the path that was only wide enough for one. Almeida for some reason didn't approach the sides of the path too much, for fear of a savage snake waiting in the tall grass. Balam and Styles as people of nations that lived and breathed snake life had no qualms walking side by side, the petals of flowers brushing his legs scenting them with the past. The birds tweeted and the mice ran occasionally in the distance running for cover from the beaten path.

Whenever Styles heard the singular blast of locust he sweated a little. For now in his mind he had attached the sound of locusts with the captivity of otherwise free men. He looked up at the sky towards the blistering sun. Thinking of all the men women forced to work the Earth as he walked free. He thought of the girl making the fire the day before and the ridiculous life she was being forced to live. Then as he walked ever closer to the statue stranger it dawned on him, that today for the first time that he could remember, he had not looked upon the sun within its first hour of rising. The sun was sacred to him, no more than the Earth and never the less. The moon could inherit all mistrust if he had any. As they walked together they came across a Boa snake. Instead of trapping the serpent, they walked curved into the grass stepping around the perimeter giving it wide berth. Back on track they continued to walk cautiously observing the ground for snakes as they went.

The mountain ahead, with its dressed lady silhouetted summit ever more dominating the panorama ahead. The light from the sun sprayed the side of the stained Panther's face, staring out across the landscape, off towards the east. Akin to Lion Mountain with its gaze fixed upon the east towards the arrivals, like Styles. The features were felinic, as though there had once been a race of Chiant cat people who set out across the world. Styles kept his gaze upon the head of the felinial statue, having scanned the last mile of ground with his acute sight. A few mice locusts and lowly creepers skittled ahead but that was it.

The three walkers side by side took in the masterful

interior of the Island. Black ebony and yellow Takamata palms graffiti'd the base of the mountain base. If it had just been a mountain Styles could have dismissed the trees as young accompanying protectors of secrets. The large impossible statue of a cat person effortlessly dominating the mountain as its own, begged questions to be asked. They were roughly half a kilometre away from the mountain, when suddenly the air got lighter and colder. The trees at the base of the mountain in comparison were that of the grass to them. "What can any of you tell me of this place?" Balam raised his eyebrows as if to say he didnt know anything". Almeida pushed his lips together licking them from inside of his mouth "When the Europeans first came here and set up the Dutch East India Company about 200 years ago, they killed who they needed until the whole population was interbred and placed in to slavery." Balam grunted as if to clear his throat. Styles looked at him and paused remembering how he had been when Sawyer spoke of the destruction of Balam's homelands.

Styles understood, but needed to know more whether Balam like it or not. "Please Senior tell me some, go on." Almeida who quite obviously was thinking about the events that had transpired cut short them continued the touchy subject. "When the Dutch came and set up government, it was run by the newly formed Dutch East India Company. The made Pieter Both Governor General of this Company. When Pieter first set eyes on this mountain and saw the magnificent Giant that you see here now. He renamed the mountain Pieter Both". Balam and Styles looked at each other and then quickly away towards a tree stump then in the direction of the mountain trying not to smile. Styles faired better he looked directly at Senior Almeida "What was the original name of this place?"

"That I do not know. There is much talk of black and white magic on this Island. Balam who was now under control of his face muscles interjected "If the original inhab-

itants could tell you I'm sure they would, but I fear they have all been assimilated by the... Europeans." Almeida looked at Balam, he could see Balam meant no disrespect it was just how things were. Styles didn't worry. As if to make things whole again, Almeida added "They say that that when Pieter Both relinquished his position, he left to return home. Of the four ships that left, two of them ship-wrecked off the coast of Mauritius,
He being on board drowned..." Styles nodded his head as if justice had indeed been served to the insane human. "Whether that is true or not I highly doubt, for there is a rhyme around these parts, I did not take the time to trans-late the entirety but remember this.

To be cruel in life
Is to pay the ultimate cost
Men drowned at sea
Ever found in paradise lost

The Dutch East India Company to this day holds the Spice monopoly throughout this region. All of the Islands are owned by them. The current Governer-General is Jeremiah van Riemsijk. From what I hear he has an affinity for the wildlife. Though doesn't understand the things here. This tree here, for example - resting unsuspectingly with its brothers and sisters below the mountain - which the first ruler named after himself. This tree is called a Takamaka, it has many healing properties in its sap. There have been long held beliefs here that the sap promotes good health and is good for the skin. The sacred pink pigeons here live in within its canopy high on the drugs within." Styles wasn't sure on the translation but he understood it to mean the pigeons were ingesting drugs like Nipnip back home. It was beginning to seem the whole animal kingdom knew no better than to enjoy the labours of nature. The walk had taken no more than two hours, Almeida took a drink but did not slow his pace or breath, he should of.

As the day passed on the three came upon the southern most point of the mountain now known as Pieter Both. Little was known of the past of the cat like creature that now stood solemn. Almeida professed to the two that they were at the meeting point. Sawyer would arrive in a few hours, travelling from Rodriguez. Then all together they would set out for Port Louis, returning to the ship as a whole crew again.

The takamaka trees made a perfect site for their camp as they waited for their voyaging accomplice. The afternoon came and all waited for Sawyers arrival. Nothing said of where or how he would arrive. It seemed only Sawyer and Almeida knew those details. Almeida checked his position using map and compass. Upon the time of day, the sun had moved passed its zenith. He took it to be 2 O'clock in the afternoon. Almeida sat upon a tree stump. The only one that Styles could see. Resting on it he stared off in to the distance. Balam stood crossing Almedia's view looking out to the west further on down the path surveying for any new Mauritians. Styles who growing more impatient in a low calm voice said "What do we do now?"

Almeida did not look up or respond. Balam who seemed to know Almeida's moods and mannerisms said "Now we wait, until Sawyer arrives. When he does, we will press on." Almeida looked up at the two of them. "Balam I have a better idea. Why don't you wait here for Sawyer? I will take Styles here to see what he can make of this mountain, should only be an hour or so okay."

Balam having not much choice in the matter agreed. Almeida stood up from the large tree stump and walked round the back of it. Styles noticed that behind the tree stump was another one further up the mountain. The terrain was level for a few hundred metres and every now and again there was another odd tree stump. Almeida walked the path of dead trees without saying a word. Styles followed. Balam continued to stair down the road towards the west.

As the two walked closer and closer to the foot of the mountain, following the tree stumps as a guide, they arrived at the cliff face. "If the mountain had indeed been a statue then between the feet of the muse would be" A lowly box was a cabin that had only recently been built. The trees that made the cabin were large and resembled the stumps that covered the ground on the way. There was nobody in the vicinity and the cabin looked to be out of use. There were no visible windows or doors. Styles looked at Almeida perplexed.

"Why have we came here?"'

Almeida did not reply. He felt he was at odds with stupidity. He walked to the side of the cabin, Styles followed. Then Styles realised the optical illusion he now saw before him. The cabin all though at the front was about 6 metres wide the length stretched 20 metres back, until the rock of the mountain touched the wood cabin. Towards the end of the cabin there looked to be a door. Still no windows were in sight and if it was a place someone lived it was definitely a dreary place.

They walked on, at which point Almeida reached to the back of his neck revealing not very nutritious looking silver chain. After unclipping and palming it he pointed towards the small hole in the middle of the door. Fiddling with it the cabin door opened. As he peered inside the darkness absorbed his vision. Almeida opened his leather bag taking out a white cloth bag. He shook it back and forth to reveal a light. He then took a step inside the long cabin. Styles intrigued followed.

Once inside Almeida shut the door. The light from Almeida was greenish yellow, the light of which only just met the wooden beam ceiling above him. As the kept walking forward it became apparent that they were walking into the mountain. The cabin was a device to stop people entering. As they walked a hundred metres or so into the base of the mountain, the mood changed. Where there had been no vibrations or feelings to speak of, Styles felt now in droves. Like the feeling he had descending the sapphire causeway back home. Styles took this cave for basalt or granite. "Almeida this feels strange"

"Hush now Styles do not worry,"

"Almeida there is something wrong. " Styles lost for more words, slowed his pace over three steps until he held the wall to on his right. As he did the resonance from the island affected his motor functions. He fell over and slowly passed out. The light of Almeida disappearing as the man left the aborigine carelessly lying in a mountain cave for who knows what reason.

Styles found himself immediately in a place he knew to be the dream world. There was no sky to speak of, only greys and he took that to be the dreaming. He was in the same tunnel that he had been only now he had no feelings of sickness and felt light. He could see Almeida clearly and there was no need for the tribo-luminescence that Almeida held in his hand. The feeling that he wasn't supposed to be there increased, even though he felt no pain upon his body. When he looked around he found that on the floor behind him was his own body slumped on the ground.

All along the walls of the cave were scratched writings of different people of different language and writing types. Some small, others large and explicative facts he did not understand. He knelt down to himself on the floor and found there to be no response. Scared to go any further in to cave with the human who was turning further and further away. Hunched and never waning further in to the grotto of bad vibes. He decided that he would instead leave the cabin and try to get help. He began to think of leaving the cave and found that the walls blurred. He found himself back in the cabin almost instantly. With the next thought of seeing Balam he was no longer in the cave, but with a blur of green and light he was instead only yards from Balam. It was as if his eyes were closed and he were screaming only to reopen them and see the world around him. It was weird.

Balam was staring at the path and listening. Seeing nothing but Mauritius he turned his attention towards the stumped trees and where his companions had left him. For just a second he thought he could see something out off the corner of his eye. When he turned his head he saw nothing. He went across to the tree stump, which now stood with new meaning. Every now and again he could feel eyes upon him, but whenever he turned his gaze he would see nothing other than trees and light. A macaque monkey could be heard in the bushes behind him. He didn't let that bother him. Then he heard multiple foot steps behind.

Before turning he said "I Bet he's Da!". The words trailed off as a fast bash to the mouth with a rock knocked him back. Hitting the ground blood trickled from his head to the boucle d'orielles growing from the ground. Balam looks up toward the attacker seeing a blur. From out of the hazy images another rock crashed down to the face in the hands of dark clothed man. A crucifix hangs around his neck. Life drained from his body. The air became light. The sensation of floating left as quick as a flash. In the same moment waking up in his own body. Belly bursting and pressure asserting rhythmically as the moments passed. He was being dragged by someone with a glowing cloth bag. He tried to speak, but only a blurb comes out. Almeida replied "You're not much good in these tunnels now are you I'm not sure what happened down there was a tunnel down to the underground".

Styles said "Put me down" Almeida did not listen and continued "There is a tunnel that leads to the southwest of this island. Someone has been syphoning of the crystals down there. I saw explosives down there". Styles burped and then continued "Put me down, Now." Almeida listened this second time and threw him as if he was a small cat. " Styles hits the ground and scraped his leg. Almeida shone the light in Styles' face

"Can you walk? "

He got up and they walked out of the tunnel back in to cabin. Once out in the open light again, Styles threw up. Almeida noticed the strange waste " Well that looks like someone who didn't drink enough water after consuming white gold". Styles looked at Almeida but said nothing. "They took Balam. Almeida caught off guard laughed." What? Who took Balam?" He turned and ran in the direction of the stumped trees. Styles shouted and began to run. "The priest".

As the two hurtled towards the final tree stump Almeida realised Styles was telling the truth. Eyes wide he searched round not seeing much. Styles knelt down facing the tree stump where Balam had been sitting. "Look at this blood, its his, its Balams.." Almeida trying to keep up with what had progressed.

"How did you know he had been taken, did something happen in the tunnels?"

"I felt strange in the tunnel I had a vision, I was back out here and I was looking through Balam's eyes, seeing what he saw." There was a pause as the resonance of Balam stung his nerves.

"I was. He was sitting there, then out of no where someone came along and hit him with a rock." Styles rubbed his face feeling for a cut or bruise but only had a tingling sensation. "We have three choices, as far as I can see. We wait here for Sawyer. He turns up we leave and head back to the boat. The second is we set off to find Balam and hope there is a trail. We risk losing Sawyer. The third is we wait here for Sawyer, and you go back in to the tunnel and 'see' if you can find Balam again."

"The third option is the only option for with the other two we risk losing both of them. We cannot allow that to happen. So I propose you get back in that tunnel and don't come out until Sawyer arrives". It wasn't that he didn't trust the Captain, but it had been his idea to have Balam wait alone and now it again he was asking Styles to go back in to the tunnel alone, these actions were not those of a good man. Almeida looked at Styles with a piercing look "Don't you think If wanted this I would have left you there in the tunnel, or sold you to the slave market." He had to admit the Captain was right, he had ample opportunity to get rid of him and he had not.

"Ill go back in there. It wont take that long for me to find him."

An hour later Almeida went in to the tunnel to retrieve Styles, stepping in the vomit on the ground. Styles looked weak. He sat on the flat ground out the front of the cabin. "Well what happened" peering in to the distance checking for Sawyer's arrival. " They are at a lake, a clear blue lake, which is higher altitude than here. The sun is behind the lake and there are 3 men with him. Its the priest from yesterday." Suddenly a tree cracked near where Balam had been taken. Both entering stealth mode they quickly skated the perimeter of the first tree stump. When they arrive they found Stan and two sailors named Wisha and Glover, after introductions, Almeida explained that the priest has taken Balam to a clear blue lake. Stan told him. 'We followed the priest from Mahebourg after you three left. Speaking to the locals it seems the priest performs exorcism.

The locals, very brutally of course, fear if we divvent quick step he will be gone. Before we have a chance to reclaim him. Its a good 20 kilometres from here". Styles did not hate Stan or anything. Only the way he spoke, he found him to be a person who had seen a lot. Neither stopping it nor accelerating it. What world did he live in? What world had he found himself in? He didn't say much, he just tried took the stare off the two sailors.

"We will set off in search of Balam. Wisha and Glover will wait here until Sawyer returns. Then we will all rendezvous at Port Loius on the north west of the island. By tomorrow night I expect get off this Island". Stan gave Wisha and Glover instructions to wait no longer than 12 hours out of ear of Senior Almeida. Then the team of three (Styles Stan and Almeida) set off north towards the Balam and the hazardous circumstances he had found himself in.

Styles wondered why they all didn't have weapons or defensive items at least. What they would do when they surely caught up with the Christian priest?

Thick forest lined either side of the road, they could see the lake Stan spoke of and Styles it seemed. His reputation was on the line. Miles and miles of sugar plantations, where enslaved people sang their songs of freedom. All remained silent sticking to the path. They at least had a cover from the view of the multitudes of people sing their Sega in choir. Two thirds of the way the volcanic mountain and the trees formed an impenetrable barrier. "I say we go left, the ground here looks trampled and I'd say if Balam is hurt he's gonna be tired by about now". Styles and Stan agreed. Fluffy white clouds were gathered above. "Id say its gonna rain soon we should press on. At the end of the field a large dolmen stood lonely as if observing its friends. The path snaked into the trees ahead rising, climbing. On they walked looking for signs of Balam and his kidnappers. The path continued for hours, snaking and winding higher and higher, until the path stopped. The ground below them had become hard as stone.

As they walked on passing the tree line, the whole area buzzed with electricity in o the ears of all three of them. They were at best a couple of hundred metres above sea level and the pressure of that would account for it. After the three acknowledged that they all felt a strange intense buzzing in the ears, Almeida asked Styles "Do you feel anything else here, " Styles said nothing at first, he could see the tree line made a large circle and their was no vegetation within. He walked forward in to the circle passed the trees and on to the soil. "Come here for everything is ok. " Styles couldn't believe his eyes. The whole ground was miraculous soils of different colours. Each separated like the seven colours of the rainbow.

Almeida entered next protected by Stan checking behind him with a hand cannon he had kept at his right hip. "Stan have you ever seen such a marvellous assortment of metals?". Styles knelt down and felt his hand in to the soil where purple and yellow streams of fine earth swirled. He took a handful. Amazed to see that the same spiral pattern descending in to the soil. Forming larger smalls as it went. Stan took samples filling a hemp satchel with handfuls of all the different coloured soils. Once he was sure to have collected all the soil they crossed over the large circle. Footprints and drag marks could be seen faintly. Left from Balam most probably.

Walking over the soils towards the treeline again they all looked at each other, a strange magnetism from the rainbow soils. Styles had no shoes on. The ground was teamed with power and tingling sensations and a mild wave of *déjà vu.* He was afraid to make a single sound and tip toed through the tree line. He then realised all the life stayed outside of the circle. As if the animals and plants had no wish to enter the quiet place on Earth. He looked back at the arrangement of soil. He wondered if he would ever see a place as such again.

Taking in as much as he could until they were gone. The climb continued and the path was over run with the forest. He found It was strange the ground held no seed either. The path was barren. As the day left, a handful of stars beamed overhead. The sky shone blue and the sun was yet to set.

At the end of the road, a mile away the peak of the volcanic crater egged them on. With the failures of being too slow, the ventured on. No other people in sight and the views from that point were spectacular. To the northwest the largest mountain on the island stood, bigger than Pieter Both even. It was half an hour later, on the crust of the crater when screams were heard. They ran up the incline towards the screams of Balam.

Over the hill they saw the ghostly man screaming from inside the cratered lake. A mighty scream "HAAWAAAA-AAAH" Rang in their ears. They looked over the embankment. Inspecting a little longer than the rest, Styles observed the group of men, afire, all looking down at Balam, another call to the Creator. There was no time to waste. With the intention of stopping, they ran down screaming and cursing doing all and anything to stop the madness. The dark clothed gatherers at the lake vaguely looked away from Balam. The axe swinger brought down precise chops of with his axe, each brutal chop, as sinister as the last.

The inverted words of madmen, blaspheming, on and on, Balam looked over with what was left of him bloodied and sweating. As Styles caught his gaze over the embers he noticed how peaceful Balams face was. It couldn't have been him screaming. It couldn't have been. Almeida stopped short of the fire screaming to the group of how they had wrongfully taken one of his crew and had not ran away from his master in the woods. On and on he shouted at them.

The Christian folk just walked away in line uttering words under their breath. The next few seconds were hazy for Styles he walked over to Balam sitting down next to him. As Styles was completely ignoring the killers, Stan ran over to his side pulling out his wand cannon and aiming it in the sky. Whether for a flare or to protect his them he brought it down with a mean look saying "You, you, any-one, who wants it?" The priest pleased with the outcome of Balam, turned to Senior Almeida and began to speak, never once looking at anyone.

In those seconds anything could of been said, but none of it would have sounded better than the cannon shots that popped out from Stan's hand weapon. One by one the followers of the mad monk fell, all seven of them, like thunderstones falling in the wind, the red blowing through their now cavitied heads. When all the moustaches and beards were laid out on the floor, Styles eventually looked up at the priest. Almeida had to stop Stan from unloading the last bullet on him. Styles had never felt vengeance and now it was happening. He knew the bang brought a ven-geance. A torture of sorts, but the priest was exempt from the torture of the bang. He could see the feigning power of Balam seeping in to the priest - no not the priest - into something around his neck. Styles leapt up towards the priest, instructing his temple to touch the soil with his swerving palm slap. Instantly bringing another blow the forehead and a third blow he palmed at the throat clutch-ing the silver necklace.

Almeida and Stan would have wanted Styles to finish the man off, but it wouldn't have served them any good. They pulled Styles away and set the priest on the ground guarded by Stan. Styles looked back at Balam. Poor Balam's body took up almost ten feet as it was sliced up in to sec-tions. Light sponged mist gathered in the middle of the lake. Styles picked up Balams two feet and placed them on his neck. Then he picked up his shins and put them on his chest. Then his kneecaps, he put them at the side of his torso. The thighs he picked up one by one and placed them on top of the shins. He then picked up the hands and with them picked up Balams penis which they had also cut off, he placed that as close to the lower torso as possible. The forearms came to rest under the neck. Balams red cape which lay underneath him had not changed shade one bit. The dye was a perfect match to the colour of his blood. Stan went to help Balam, as he wrapped up the body inside of the cape.

Almeida put his arm out to stop Stan from doing so. Once the sack was over Sytles' shoulder he walked in to the lake taking his short-lived friend in to his resting place. Once in the centre of the lake he took in a large breath and descended as far as he could on one breath.

Once the heinousness of the situation had become apparent in the murkiness of the waters he untied the sack and the 17 pieces of Balam spilled out slowly, two pieces a time, falling deeper and deeper in to the bottomless lake. He thought for a moment of Balam and how what had happened could just of easily of happened to him. He couldn't find the mental strength to tell his hand to release the red cape. How could he? In his other hand the silver necklace he had taken from the priest, with the two gems of Balam attached. Without thinking he climbed higher and higher back towards the surface world. As he did the cape hugged his shoulders and the locket came to be in the inside seams of the Balams Cape interior breast pocket.

After a slow swim back to shore, the priest who had made off, only to sit in the distance watching the aborigine deal the last death to the remnants of Balam's body. Stan and Almeida found it weird to see Styles stood there looking at a black man who now reminded them of a younger version of they're central American friend. As Styles looked down he could see the purple and light mist that had been on the lake now vapored from his clothes. Almeida and Stan didn't seem to notice for if they did they might of commented on the other worldly ether that waved from the fabric.

"Can we go now Senior Almeida, if that is all" The snappishness of his tone was not entirely unexpected. The attack on the priest had been and had it not been for Almeida's high status he might of received punishment for such an attack on a man of the cloth. Yet Almeida too, had hateful feelings towards this priest, looking at Styles who a more superior man of the cloth " I don't care if you did, that priest had it coming, Company island or not, I don't like it, what happened to Balam was wrong, so wrong. I say we get out of here I don't want to spend a moment here longer than I have to, its a damn shame.

If we stay here another night who knows what might happen, I say we get back to the ship and wait for Sawyer there". There was no argument. The priest waited for them to leave in the northwest direction, then went to the bodies laid out like pointless sardines. Having checked the pockets of the dead, he scuttled off over the east way. Like a crafty vulture circling it's pray seeing where they end up without actually manning up.

Pelting down the side of mountain leaving the unforgivable lake behind. Styles wondered how much longer it would be until they would reach the Vessel and be gone. There was no need to speak. No time to process what had happened. Bringing their feet off the soil and putting them down was all the signals they needed to relay to each other. They simply would wait another night. On they ran, one, two, three kilometres down the hill making a left for the north east coast. Going as fast as the boulders and bushes would allow.

Arriving at a little settlement called Phoenix the three of them slowed their pace. It was maybe another three kilometres to Port Louis. They arrived in the prairie of a large two large houses. Surrounded by the hazy greys and light browns of sugar canes. The path led directly between the two. Two men sat on a veranda of a house. The sun had barely moved position since they had descended the mountain as if it waited for them.

The men stood up, then walked slowly to them gathering pace. Then all at once, ran across the lawn toward the three. "Et vous monsieurs pourquoi vous est pas avec le St Francois d'Assis?" Stan responded directly with words although keeping an eye on Almeida behind him so that the man could not see him draw his gun if needed to. "Qui est cet homme?" The man apparently a follower of "The priest the priest, you speak English?"

Styles looked down at his robe that was still wet and drenched in the blood of Balam. It glistened with the last of the rays of the sun. Yet the original colour served its purpose well he thought to himself.

"This slave was baptised by Monsier D'Assis, he should have been exe... erm... exorcized" Almeida stepped forward. "There was! Two of my navigators when I arrived here, one was clothed in red and the other was not . The clothed one was baptised and executed. The other is the man you see here who wears the cloth of the dead man in some kind of respect I can only admire. "Show him Styles!" The red caped aborigine gripped the fabric rinsing the blood of Balam in to his fingers, wet with the lake of Grand Basin of Mauritius. He flicked it perfectly across the potbelly of the foul-mouthed human. "For would you do a thing as that for your fellow man? Does it even mean anything to you?" Almeida was getting louder by the second. It was obvious he would not stand any more from the insolent followers of the so called 'Saint'.

"That may be the case. That may not be the case. This man could be the one due an exorcism, and he might not, for we will leave you here now and go find our priest. for god's law rules us and all here". The men backed off as he spoke only to continue around them towards the lake an all the dead men Stan had left there. "Fine go find your master, you shall find a fire and dead men, a worthy fire for you to see what the lord deems right."

The two unarmed men left leaving the three to continue their escape towards the harbour of Port Loui. They continued on down the path past the mill and well until they left Phoenix all together. The trees huddled together again until the only sign of society came as grey smoke wafting in a purple sky. The birds once again filled the air with their songs. Distinguishing themselves by swooping down on to the path ahead of them as they shrieked Big black birds, pink pigeons flew all around. Stan blew his nose. Then the other two did the same. The smell of lush untamed cannabises filled the air. Styles and Stan helped themselves to fat buds. As they ended their final road towards their final destination the rain began to trickle, spitting down towards their dirty faces. On the horizon the ocean waited for them. Their feet signals had taken them all the way to the coast of Mauritius. It was walking distance from Le Pouce. They descended on to the beach, which breathed calm majestic waves on to the white sandy shores. The sand was warm and Styles felt a slight increase in temperature rush through his body. The gold he had taken that morning was beginning to feel like a bad idea. As he had no idea who had the mix he was left wondering what its original purpose was. As he near'd the end of the stretch of the beach he saw a man working. black Mauritian stood burning pigeons on the fire he had made. He began to talk to the Senior Almeida, and he could not understand. Stan translated for the two strangers obviously taking Almeidas attire to me the man of the most wealth. There were 4 birds tied up and quite healthy about 10 feet from the fire tied up and clucking. All four were pinkish pigeons. Close to the birds a wooden crate. Styles looked in side and was surprised to see a blue one and one white. Lobster. Stan and the man spoke some more until Stan became excited at what the man had said. Then the black man took the four birds and gave them to Styles handing him the cord which was attached to all four. The man then took the two lobsters and placed tem inside a white pillow case handing them to Stan. Almeida looked on towards Pouce until they were ready to leave. Stan opened his purse and gave the man two coins which did not look very nutritious.

Looking out to sea Styles thought about the leviathan he had seen while on the Vessel. It was out there still moving calmly watching. After helping Senior Almeida choosing to carry the pigeon as opposed to the lobster. The three of them continued up the beach. Over that cliff is Port Louis, tis only a few kilometres away, come on let's do this'. Seeing as the beach ended abruptly they were forced to gain higher ground and walk the cliff tops. Smoke fires burnt a mile in land and they passed a long road that lead back to the interior of the island.

They stood at the end of the road where it met the coast. A small path made from foot prints and slow walks had had two wooden posts united by a plaque that read 'Port Loui 2km' with an arrow pointing left. Someone had tagged the sign to read VOSTFR. What did it mean? The French were using Sub Titles. Not High Titles like the Originals? or the Versions? Back on the Vessel he'd heard Loui talk about the VOSTFR. The town with the fire smoking behind the arrow had no sign post and the long wide road was unmarked it seemed. Behind them. The Pieter Both Mountain range with it's four peaks looked to them as statue's rising in to the skies. In its middle stood the Statue of the Cat Man. Its head bold and wise. It was then that they heard and explosion. It sounded like the awakening of a volcano, or the opening of a cloud through force of lightning. The base of Pieter Both exploded. Dynamite.

Almeida explained to Styles "Quickly We must go now. They have sealed off the cave entrance at the base of Pieter Both. We must arrive at the Port Loui and hope that Sawyer has made it back. For I now know that it was all connected, the priest, the explosion, even the two men we met at Phoenix. I will explain all later but now we must make haste. On they went in the direction of the sign post. Beautiful flowers lined the sides of the path.

Patterns of yellow and red blurred the sides of the walk-way. Backdrops of green. The sun now set. Pigeons agitated by speed of the journey grunted and fluttered their wings unable to do much else but hope to be free again. Styles felt for the bird and as they neared closer to the peak of the cliffs he finally saw the madness that was Port Louis. It dwarfed the oddly named Grand Port and for good reason. More people were trying to be hidden here and so arriving at a Grand Port would not be the most secretive of plays. As they ventured closer Almeida began to stair out towards the harbour checking to see the Vessel. Among the array of tall ships, clippers and galleons he saw the Vessel even in the night sky. A Maltese flag hung at half mast to continue the guise of friendship with the colonists. Stan coughed har and brought something up from his throat spitting it to the ground. The area around the port was busy with life. River inlets approached, bridges of wood lay over them. To the north of Port Loui a large gardens covered the land-scape, beyond that a church. Its tower top pinnacling out over the trees. The second dirt road in to port loui from the north east was full of Mauritian's chained in irons on their heads and feet. All were being marched towards the church square. Almeida explained "As the Vessel floats at the far northern end of harbour we have to walk very close to the slave market." From what Styles could gather the slaves were captured from the inlands of Mauritius.

Almeida walked ahead with the authority his robe and emblem on his shoulder acquired him. As Styles walked at the back with Stan he asked questions that could help him understand the history of what he saw before him. Stan in no round about way began to explain as best he could. The wind blew from Almeida to him and so quietly he spoke. "The men and women who had lived on the island for no less that the past 1500 years had settled there after arriv-ing from a place near Saudi Arabia. The people had lived peacefully having decided to leave their homeland with a fleet of of 60,000 people. While this enormous fleet had circumvented Africa a small group of them had settled Mozambique on the East coast of Africa a thousand or so. From there they arrived in Madagascar by ship and also the islands surrounding that include Mauritius. The arrival of the Europeans two centuries before had only brought war with them."

When Styles tried to dig further and asked why the people simply didn't take back their lands, Stan told him that even though the original people of Mauritius had been placed in to slavery and even though they were forgetting that they originally inhabited the island, there were signs all over the Earth that would make sure the true history of the peoples of Earth would never be lost entirely. No matter how hard the Future Makers tried. Not much more was said after that on the subject. It was obvious to Styles that Stan was a good man. Though he had an issue telling the truth (to Styles especially when around other humans). It was as if he carried a guilt that could only be expunged by professing the truth to Styles. If that was the true reasoning behind Stan's motives than so be it he thought to himself. 'For at least I will be wiser for it'. "Hush now for you will surely be heard among the men here). Skirting the perimeter of the harbour wise to not go directly in to it. No matter what the temptation. It was not just thieves and robbers that had entered from Europe they had to worry about. The road they came upon was sign posted with the same craftsmanship as the sign for Port Louis. It was dirtier and the ground around was trampled beyond mere slow walking. Cart tracks and and heavy feet had felt the ground. It wasn't surprising that Styles again to feel bad. The sign post simply read. "Cimetière de l'église Francoise d'Assise'. The church yard displayed remnant of slave trading. Though that was all. "No more baptism's" Styles said.

"This church was built around the time of your birth Styles, in honour of a Saint known as Francois." Stan stayed silent. Styles saw the connection with the sign post. In the church yard. There were the clothes of a man who no longer needed them. They had been placed upon crucifix that towered over the rest of the graves. It had been position so as to scare off the birds who might pick at the remnants of deep people, who were sometimes slaughtered for whatever reason a slave master could think of. Out of the kneck of the garment the crucifix masked with a balaclava. To give the demeanour of something alive and intelligent. were still upon the graves.

Almeida knocked on the door, tapping three times. After a minute or so a priest answered the door, saying nothing but allowing Senior Almeida to enter. The door again closed and it was minute or so before it opened again. When it did it was left open and Styles was surprised to Sawyer coming out of a trap door at the end of the church floor. Closing marble floor piece. The monk had merely been careful making them wait before entering. The monk had on a robe which didn't seem to fit him around the legs, it was if the man had grown to large for his Habit.

Sawyer closed the trapdoor. As he did the priest closed the door surveying the clothes upon the crucifix in the churchyard. No sooner had Sawyer picked up his two bags, which lay at either side of the trap door and they were off again out the door. The monk said nothing to any of them and they all left following Almeida's lead. All left the church. Styles looked at the clothes fleshing the crucifix gravestone in the yard. The jumper was of a dark grey colour and looked warm to wear. The trousers were grey and long, a good fit for the monk he thought.

As they went on, the pigeons continued to grunt and the lobsters snapped occasionally to the sound of nothing. Sometimes they waited at the end of the paths, zig-zag'ing bushes through the churchyard. They were not in the mood to get stopped by anyone. All that mattered was getting away from the island.

As they left the churchyard, it was seconds before they could the noise of a quarrel back at the door of the church. Men's voices, Onomatopoeias

of surprise. Onward the crew hurried towards their Vessel. Through a botanical garden, pausing for cover, Stan picked Hibiscus flowers and placed them in his satchel. Once out of the beauty they made their way across the cliff side, on from the men in the churchyard, towards the Harbour.

They were now 50 metres from the Vessel. Silently the four of them navigated their way down a steep bank. One by one they slid, down the bank. Stan fell in the mud tumbling a few of steps before regaining his stance. It was quiet on the dock, apart from music coming from one of the large East India ship.

Ready to be filled with Mauritian captives. One by one they boarded the Vessel. First Stan then Sawyer followed by Styles and lastly Almeida. By the time the guards of the port arrived at the dock, it was too late. The Vessel had left the harbour. Hope of sending a ship to retrieve them was useless. Looking out towards the Vessel the guards stood staring, cursing the windy waters.

STYLES AND ISLE SANTE MARIE

The master mariners sailed closer to southern shore of Isle Sante Marie. For some unknown reason someone had forgotten to use the compass. Whether someone had unintentionally detoured or not, it would never be known.

However, it seemed the maps had been used and they arrived at the southern shore of Sante Marie. The sun lingered in the north, taking its time to drop below the horizon. The skies were clear and the sea air blasted the deck. The waters all around the Vessel spiralled like the end vortexes. Humpback whales endangered the sides of their magnificent ship. Most of the crew had focused their eyes westwards as the largest of the whales leapt in to the sky.

It was blocking the access to the island of Sante Marie. The drenched whale flopped in to the waters, rocking the ship enough for those at the back of the ship to hold on tighter than usual.

"ALL HANDS ON DECK" Sawyer shouted. They had entered the fringes of the notorious island that was known to be the most successful pirate outpost the Indian ocean had ever seen. Inventions from VIndia's past had wobbled their ways over the waters and the first instance of this was heard in the shape of a cannon ball leaving the shores of Sante Marie towards the unwelcome travellers on their beloved Vessel.

The cannon ball shot through the air swerving past the main mast on to the brim behind them splashing a Whale.

Styles was sure that the ball had hit the sea creatures. He worried more for them than the crew he had found himself among. A call was made for a magic flag to be raised. A few moments later a white flag with yellow arches was raised. Once raised and tightened in to position Almeida called for the foghorn to be sounded. Another cannon ball shot passed rupturing the smallest sail. A sailor close to the rig slipped off freefalling to the Vessel below. Styles watched as the crew ran around untightening the ripped sail until it slumped closer to the deck.

The vortexes of the Whales all swirled one last time and left the humans to continue their array of relays. The whales, tired of the games the men had found themselves in. A foghorn sounded from the shore, half a kilometre away. Then the mood of all the crew mellowed.

Loui, Theau and Leo yelled out cheers of joy having avoided being submerged so close to the end of their voyage across the lonely seas between Mauritius and Madagascar. Styles caught the eye of Senior Almeida coming down the step at the front of the Vessel staring at him.

The carpenter came out of the cabin door with a small stretcher for the sailor lying on the deck. A sailor had fallen twenty feet and only managed to pop his shoulder out of place and bruised his face. The upper body strength of the crew was a testament to work needed to work the Vessel. Two sailor's helped the carpenter get the man below deck.

The man stood up defiantly. With the one arm that still worked he motioned for people to back off. His face twisted, he walked towards the cabin door. The carpenter acted more like a doctor than carpenter of ships. A man shouted down from up high "Oh, Loui faire attention". The man who had fallen stopped walking, turned and looked up and said "AY- TEO Ferme ta guele". Pointing to the cabin door. "Ah Muddy Garcon!" was the reply from up high.

Obviously vexed, the carpenter looked up towards the young crewman. He took aim and through thin air at the two jokers. Theau who knew the old man's game, smiled still. The lad with him turned his gaze at the last moment to see the carpenter throw something, but wasn't thoroughly sure what it was. He took protective action and almost fell backwards protecting himself - trying to evade a thunderstone that existed in his mind. Built and put there by the wise carpenter.

Sante Marie Island absorbed the Vessel even though the sail was full of holes. The sun had not set and that was good for all aboard.

The canon fire from the Island stopped. The arches on the flag must have helped. Somewhere high on that island laid a sweet victory. One by one all went below deck, returning in attire appropriate for the madness that was to come.

Styles had been prepared long before he arrived on deck. The red cape modified - wafted in the wind - behind him. Onward he gazed to parody of paradise, but it was not his. No need for any Captain to tell him to prepare for what laid ahead of him. Always in his mind now, it was to be wary - unless, he wanted to be dead too. Even with the cape pulled back over his shoulders, his dragon fly eye was no match for the etheric warbs coming from his dead friends garment.

Thankfully, to the untrained onlooker his squinting eye could be attributed to many things. Apart from himself nobody on board could see the blinding light that blared from the seams of the cape, where he had torn the cape in half.

The line he imagined shone all the way down his back. Balam was still dead in the water and so Styles would wear his cloth. He had used Balam's crystal to cut the cape. It only covered his left shoulder, now flowing down to his feet. Still he could feel the light, as if it only light up the unforeseen. As the sun set they made their way closer to the bay of Sante Marie. Now at night when the sun went low below the horizon, all eyes on deck noticed the cape of Balam.

Word had got round to most of the crew of the untimely death of the Balam man of the Cholula people in Mexico. The Vessel was an incubator for the love of the unknown. Even the new members of the crew had heard what had happened. Styles had somehow inherited the place, which was previously Balam's. He didn't like the way he was the only black person now aboard the Vessel.

He didn't know what to make of it, but here he was, voluntarily with them he thought to himself, as if to re-assure his mind. Boatswain Stan reappeared, followed by a crew of 2 men, getting to work on repairing the sail. Senior Almeida appeared dressed in black. His cloak covered all items and weapons he carried and he stood prepared. Side by side and one by one eyes gazed upon the Island.

If it wasn't for the warning shot the island might of been considered home to one of the most beautiful beaches an island could have. Lanterns shined on the white sands. Exotic birds took flight from the palms climbing high over the greenery of Sante Marie. The crew marvelled at its beauty, all but Stan.

He shouted for Wisha who was nowhere to be seen. Theau and Leo worked as best they could to keep up with the orders that came bellowing from Stan on how to change a sail. It seemed they would have to dock in order to really do a good job. All realised the truth. As long as they had a problem with the sail, they could only drift to the clutches of the most notorious pirate hideout since Zanzibar.

As eyes watched from the dock of Sante Marie Styles could feel something in the air. His instinct was telling him beyond any doubt that the entire crew were fearful. As the crew hurried back and forth it was clear. They all clung to the hope of a swift visit. In and out before the true identity of the Vessel could be known.

Sawyer straight faced took a register of all the crew. All but one person was accounted for - Wisha. Theo and Leo worked on the repairing the sail to the dismay of two large birds nesting on the moon mast. As the ship docked Stan kept screaming "Wisha Man!"

The emerald waters surrounding the Vessel shimmered. Styles clocked the eyes of the girl on the dock, as did most. Almeida seemed to recognise her or the scar on her face. He stamped his foot once on the deck. Surely a tell tale sign he had been here before?

The two shouted back and forth as the ship docked from ship to shore. Almeida kindly shouted, "What is a girl like you doing in a place like this?" (His tone was calm and oblivious.) The girls eyes widened and a fury rose up in to every particle of her face. Then as the girl looked at the Vessel's flag flapping with the yellow arches, her face softened once more.

"Sir you seriously tell me you do not know my heart bleeding story of the East India Company leading me to this desolate existence." Her smile revealed itself for the first time. Twisted with the experience of the reality of being a powerful woman in the brutal clutches of a mad world.

As the Vessel's plant was stretched out to the wooden dock a wave of peace flowed over the ship. A feeling brought on by the thought to be in a place where the absolute tyranny of slavery no longer lingered. Almeida stomped his foot down on the deck twice more. The board creaked followed by a muffled scream from below deck, followed by the banging of large pans.

Sawyer walked towards the cabin door laughing to himself, just as the cabin door bust open, spitting out Wisha standing dressed in black and carrying a hammer, with hair covering his face. Following protocol he went to his post near Stan, trying to blend in. He was careful not to make eye contact with either Almeida or Sawyer.

From the dock, a woman looked at Styles. Momentarily looking at his hair. Wisha coughed and then looked up. The woman glanced his way and the fury returned to her face. As the girls eyes squinted, her face was one of fact. This girl knew Wisha. Styles could feel time slowing down, but only for her. Memories flooded her mind and all the crew all stood now watching her, even Sawyer. Almeida being quite slow to catch on to any of this offered a smile and some light conversation. The girl it seemed was actually a woman who was ignoring Almeida's broken English.

The woman eyed all the crew one by one. Her face, full of beauty and warmth. To stop herself breathing heavily, her eyes gazed up towards Theo and the higher parts of the ship. Still her demeanour was like an armed combatant. As the moments passed her mannerisms leavened once more. The Vessels flag seemed to calm her. They were for sure at Sante Marie. Styles heard Theo say. "Sante Marie avais de mayor introduction, beh oui ce class."

As Stan left the Vessel followed by Almeida, they were greeted with a sincere apology for the attack on their Vessel. The woman's voice grew louder when offering hospitality so that all crewmembers could hear her. "You are all to be received by the head of the Island the Kid Clan." Almeida gave his permission with a glance and accented response.

"I accept though some of my crew shall remain aboard, as repairs to the sail are needed, we mean not to dock and to stay longer than need be." The woman nodded dying to speak.

"The fact that you have the white and Yellow arch flag means you are welcome as long as you so desire, even if in pursuit by or of any type of European Authority".

Senior Almeida pulled a handkerchief out with the house of Almeida stitched in to it. The insignia a rough outline of Malta surrounded by a large circle. The woman took it and nodded, withdrawing inland, noticing the well behaved crew.

Theo once again lightened the mood with a whistle. All looked up at him. In his best English he said "The birds will not scarper". Once off the dock and parallel to the mid-section of the Vessel, the girl turned looking directly at Wisha, waiting to exchange a glance. When he looked up it was directly at her. Seconds passed - more than enough for her to recognise his face. Although her meeting of the Vessel at the shore of Nosy Boroha was unexpected, the crew were granted permission to leave the Vessel. "Come" the woman said, inviting them to follow her.

Upon walking towards Pirate Town, in the company of Senior Almeida Sawyer, Styles said not a word. Three sailor's carrying bayonets and survival supplies, appeared on the path ahead of them. The woman revealed her hook hand, raising it high for the sailors to see. There was no big puzzle. Far away in the middle of the Island, a flag with similar aches to the Vessel, stood perversely proud, atop to the skyline. There were no guards at the dock, only the woman.

Following the sandy narrow footpath into the winding jungle it could of been easy to get lost, if it wasn't for the melodic whistling ahead. The group stretched their legs as they strode and took in the fresh air. The temperature was hotter than it had been on the Vessel and the forest life was similar to Mauritius. The trees filled every nook higher than 10 metres above sea level. Though Isle Sante Marie was narrower and a lot smaller, cannabis grew everywhere. Sawyer remarked to lack on Boatswain. "Good thing Stan isn't here, he'd never wanna to leave." In his best English.

"Had he the smallest inkling this magical plant life lay

here, he might have been a problem". Still and silently Styles admired the multitudes of flowers that skittled the short 5 minute walk to the entrance of a mighty fortress made of wood. The narrowing path stopped in front of 20 metres high construct.

Gridded in design, the horizontal and vertical beams made it near impossible to navigate. The woman was nowhere to be seen.

Green fruit hit the ground forcing all the crew to look up. Captain Almeida told his sailors to lower their weapons. "Tis I Senior Almeida, I am expected". With that the doors swung up in to the trees, pulled by some as yet unseen mighty force capable of lifting multiple fully grown tree trunks into the air like throwing ones hand in the air.

As the veil lifted, they all prepared for what they would encounter inside. Wood huts and cabin's populated the camp that was basic in appearance in contrast to the fortress design. Wild Orchids grew under the windows of the cabins, suiting the paradise they had found themselves in perfectly. The walls surrounding the camp were made of large tree trunks, which looked like they were mysteriously hoisted into position, towering above the huts and cabins.

The forest around the camp gripped over the tops of the wooden barricade. The branches swayed back and forth and fanned the campfire smoke as it spiralled upwards towards the sky. Three woman came out from the back of the hut directly opposite them. The fire smoke cleared and faces shone like mirages of some sort. All walked towards the warm meeting place.

For all intents and purposes, this was just a village on an island. The three were all strong, straight-backed and long-haired, with their hair tied in pony tails. One of the women started yelling in a loud warm voice, the other two women looked over as if she had spoilt the moment, with her mood altering acapella. The two other scorned her with a look that showed just how long the women had been there.

The tallest one wore a dress laced with pearls that were laced in to her fabric, hanging lavishly from her violet dress. Her tanned neck was adorned with white shells that blossomed in between curly red and yellow crystals, so many of which bushed across her chest.

The girl to her right had the same complexion yet her eyes were as dark and wide, dressed similarly in as much as her choice of accessories, but the same size dress on her, gave a more guarded demeanour. Starfish adorned her shoulders chest and hips in a way one would of thought her a mermaid. Whether orange, pink or blue the starfish were all dead, long and thin and dead. The legs of each one touched another, webbing the out line of her tight but snug waisted leather jacket. Her trousers were that of a dead man's and were rolled up to her knees. On her hips she wore something so bright it could not be seen as a weapon, yet there it was at the waist. Bulging out from her jacket like the handle of a gun was a black and gold starfish - bigger than all the other's she had killed - hardened and woven in to her fabric.

The third girl could not be explained. For to explain her would give the impression the three were sister's. The third was in fact the mother of the other two and when she spoke, the crew of Almeida knew it to be true. Styles came to the same conclusion by another means, noticing no extravagant amulets or tokens of power, instead her heart singing as a gesture to all that come afterwards.

The first woman who was from the dock, was nowhere to be seen. The dense forest and shrubs surrounding the enclosure were perfect for hiding. Pirates most likely more lived in the woods than they did in the actual camp. Natural alarms guarded the entrance at night in the shape of dry spiky fauna. Anyone could see they were expecting more people. The map of the fortification embellished the scope of what to expect. Styles knew that at least.

Three of Almeidas men arrived on cue, lead by Kelvis who went to speak but stopped when Almeida piped up, simply coughing instead, stopping any words coming out, remembering where he was. Almeida looked down at the ground where Kelvis stood. Bags of Cannabis lay at the side of him. Seeing this, Kelvis took the bag over his shoulder. Caught in the moment and as all watched, he began to speak in his broad Yorkshire accent, trying to change the subject from what was in the bag, he said. "So Almeida. Have you spoken to the leader of the Kirates yet. That would. I mean Pirates." Noticing his two men still had their bags open and also full of cannabis, he fell silent after that and a sweat crept upon his face waiting for Senior Almeida's reckoning reply.

The Starfish jacketed woman began to speak. "I'll not have any more interruptions". Kelvis told his men to wrap the bags up and be quiet. "I am herself - the descendant of Captain William Kidd - the most notorious of all Kirates. My name is Kera" this is my sister Hallie and our mother Claire - Grand daughter of the Mr Kidd, making myself and Hallie the great grand daughters." The women neither waved nor curtseyed. There was no empress to speak of; only the magic attained in knowing these two women knew the island better than anyone. "It is rude to speak of piracy if you were not one yourself." Looking at Styles "preferring to remain elusive of any details other than that which Kelvis here would have to give myself pertaining to Almeida. Neither his status nor occupation" likewise stating he was the captain of a large 'Ship' that would be making its way back to the Mediteranean. I heard all this from my agent at yh dock.. Had you not been attacked you might be off the island". Almeida read the lines between the conversations. It felt they were stalling for time, either someone else was coming to see the or the ship was to be attacked; there was rarely a third option.

"What say you explain they ways about here so that I

might go on about was unbound, to the furthest degree possible in the vicinity of these waters of course". Being careful to neither disrespect nor empower too much, the smart women in their precarious position.

He knew just by looking at the walls of sheer tree trunks, that they themselves could not of surely hoisted these things in to position on their own. There must surely be a camp of 50 or plus men, no doubt about it, maybe this place was to just to protect the woman and children.

Hallie spoke out for the first time. As she did, Styles could help feel her aquatic future ahead of her. As if all the animals in the ocean would listen to her. Styles could see Haillie knew everything was gonna be alright. One day leaving the Island.

By the time Haillie had finished speaking in her soft voice, all had fallen under a spell. Though there was none to her mind that she could have guessed. Once again Haillie repeated. "Yes we are the descendants of the late and great William Kidd, and to the furthest extent we expect to be treated in the same manner. No this is not an Island where the French or colonialist rule matters, no this, the island where all are free. Now one of your crew there, back on the deck o'ya ship, he be a man by the name of Coulson, his father live on this Island. He has been asking for his whereabouts for almost a year now. Seems he got a girl pregnant last year and now is with baby. I nothing to a man like yourself, I can understand. But all alone you see, no one, one day she took the baby out to the shore. you see tree line to get some food, she was only gone a moment you nah, baby got snatched away like that' She clicked her finger

"Was a lemur you see, apparently one a them tall black sifikas snatched a baby away. Dear girl, awful crying mess man, when word got around, been alone all that time, expecting Coulson to come back, then to lose her baby like that. Without a trace. So I saw ya man Coulson there, even he knows and he's staying away. But I tell ya! I doubt that very much, better man be scared than know the truth, so I say he stow away on ya ship since before ya got here, maybe Mauritius, me know he got a cousin there. He is figuring to get to Madagascar, maybe further, who knows what he dreams, anything but taking care of his cares and duties as a father to his kid. Plain and simple. Hungry?"

After the Sante Marie ladies prepared a supper, the subject of attack was brought up by the two sailor's who were anxious to know if they would continue to be under attack. Clare said that the attack was only to scare anyone advancing to island. The next move of the attacker's would be to tell their group or master, in this case the brother of Kera and Hallie. They didn't mention his name, only that he would soon find out that a ship had come. He would arrive in person as early as the next morning.

Almeidas crew had become nervous. Kelvin spoke of Nightfall approaching and it being too late to leave and navigate in such conditions - Even a mere 20 miles to Madagascar and docking would be tricky. The women produced a map of the island, which was aligned differently to the map aboard the Vessel.

At the north, 30 kilometres or so was a large camp run solely by her brother and others who had learned to live on the island continuously for one hundred years. Ever since the great William Kidd and the descendants of one other crewmember called Coulson. As they spoke of Coulson again, Hallie explained the gravity of his return. "If word made it back that Coulson was in the area being harboured by the Vessel, an attack would surely be made. If you stay and handed him over, it could end amicably".

To Styles the chance of anyone making it out alive knowing his experience was slim. Still captain Almeida agreed to sleep on the island, a message that would be seen as the actions of a calm person and innocent person, one who could not possibly harbour a known fugitive of pirate island Sante Marie.

Church Bells began to ring out, eleven times Styles counted. Eleven rings at a distance of 6 miles. Other women exited huts and homes with scented dolls, which they all threw on the fire. Taken for wind in the trees above rustling like a child having fun in a bush, knocked leaves downed from overhead. The silence among the men was cut now and again by the snapping of twig.

Styles undeterred by the young sailors lack of enthusiasm for the customs of the women, offered to help Kera as she matted the fire with a fan. She looked at him with a sigh, as if unaccustomed to the kindness, although she most definitely will have. Her only flaw in life was attached to the heritage of an infamous pirate.

Still the man continued to smile to himself. Her beauty encapsulated him for a time. The strangeness of the situation proceeded further when the sailor's who had knapsack, happily helped themselves to the rum bottles in one of the packs. The laughs increased as the men drank rum. After a time Almeida's serious tone mellowed and he joined the young sailors in a drink. He joked "Fortis only one bottle, not enough to kill a captain, but a sale sailor maybe."

As the bottle made it's way around the men, cautious not to offer any to the women for fear of poisoning the smoke raised up from the fire, that continued to spiral as it hit the leaves of the enclosing forest. Styles remembered the fire and dolls were talisman's to ward off bad vibes. Whether the rest of the crew knew what was up he wasn't sure. Sawyer had not touched a drop of the overpowering concoction. He stood up keeping his hands at his sides. Without warning he walked towards the entrance of the fortress as if to leave. The sailor's merry banter stopped momentarily.

Then assuming he was just taking a slash. The women realising he had not touched a drop and was trying to leave. The two women stood up and Kera spoke "Soya, Where are you off to?" Sawyer turned around facing Styles. "Are YOU coming ?" The look on his face was serious and torn. He was hiding his real face with a turn of the neck. Styles wondered for a second where Sawyer kept his real face. Without saying a word Styles stood up and walked towards Sawyer ignoring the woman. Calmly walking between the sister's feet and the fire. He was warm and glanced at Senior Almeida clutching the bottle. Just as he passed the group who sat chilling by the fire, he heard the voice of Kera cry out" Where are YOU going? Styles turned his neck to face her. His expression was hardly serious or comical but he knew if he ignored he she would let him walk.

Kera began to talk again but was stopped short by Almeida. "My dear Kera, my men are returning to the Vessel, they will relay the information that you have bestowed upon us. Mr Sawyer here is my first mate, my *numero uno*. He will tell the crew to prepare for the ship for company in the morning".

The wind blew from the noises in the fire. Her mother and sister both looking around checking that nothing else had changed. "What we have here is a case the gitters, simply release my first mate here and the good man Styles. I will remain here, as captain I will surely mean more to your brother, especially if he wants to take a member of my crew." Kera looked at the young sailors, led by Senior Almeida "I marvel at the flair in which a man could attain a future of his choosing, even when it seemed one was losing." Almeida stood up for his epic final comment. "You know it to be true, let them go, I'm sure you have eyes on the Vessel, I'm sure there is more fire left in that cannon.". He then smiled and sat back down neither drinking nor breathing. All went silent then Kera smiled and turned her face back and forth eventually looking towards her sister, raising her left eyebrow in a half moon smile.

The gates once again swung open silently. The unknown doormen high in trees were hidden from view. Listening and controlling who entered and left the pirate compound. Styles reached Sawyer and they continued toward the entrance. The sailors continued to drink caring only for their ambience around the fire. Almeida had clear reign to play his part speaking his words with the woman Kera on their ways. The mood relaxed now that they shadow known as Sawyer had left. The mother explained while standing then entering one of the wooden cabins. The charismatic night sky had matched her silence for a brief history of time until the loud shriek of a lemur called out. The sailors, although naïve, turned their comedy to the sounds of the native animals. Until Almeida calmed them by standing up and then relieving himself near the entrance. The sister's watched him walk thick booted in through the haze of the fire smoke.

As he stopped at the entrance he turned and looked over to the women, without saying a word he turned right and stopped just at the tree wall. The women turned their attention to the fire once more and the gate closed slower than it had earlier.

As the lemurs laughed Almeida imagined Styles and Sawyer walking away, the moonlight auspiciously lighting the way. The white sands below their feet, whispered. Purple and green flowers known only by scent guided the way back to the Vessel. Once aboard, welcomed by Stan, the three went below deck and waited for everything to turn silent once more.

It was the early hours of the morning when Stazn relayed that they were being watched from higher up, in the centre of the island, northwards a mile. Sawyer mentioned a plan, which Stan repeated as if taking an order. A style then repeated the word in question form, but was met with silence. "Almeida needs you now? We need to leave, me and you now, get some weapons, get whatever you need to eat, get whatever protection you might need and lets go".

When Styles arrived back on deck he was dressed in black, the same black that hung in the crew's room. The red cape lingered over his right shoulder. The dark of the night dampened the redness, he thought to himself, as he imagined how the rest of the world saw this cape. The light effect had not subsided in all the time he had been wearing it. He was sure it was somehow empowering him in a way he had not thought of. It was beginning to nag at him but subsided when Sawyer appeared from the navigation room.

No words were spoken for the two of them were too smart for that at this point. Only imperative information would pass between the two, he thought too himself. Anyone else and it might be uncomfortable for them. Not with Sawyer though, it was as if after all this time something had clicked in and he was a buzz ebbed now, where before there was nothing. It meant that they were beginning to have an effect on each other's future. That aside there was still some animosity between the two. It could hardly be helped considering the uncanny situations they found themselves in. He was still unsure how the two would do whatever it was they were about to do. He had brought with him flashes of *déjà vu*, that rushed through him giving him intense mind to speak.

Suddenly Sawyer spoke of how they would sail across the water in a small skysail boat; there was enough cloth from the broken torn sail for this 2 man mission to Madagascar. Sawyer then handed Styles the sword of oracleum that came from the Obelisk back in Astraliyah 'Use it for your life'.

Sheathing and belted under his right hip, Sawyer admired the style and his approach combat with a one handed weapon. 'For it was backwards to him and to battle someone, took such technique. It would be like fighting your mirror. Your hand and theirs would lash every time and so it would come down to balance, speed, and accuracy. The right-handed individual would be used to battling right-handed opponents, but the left-handed would also be used to fight right-handed opponents. So when a match between a right-handed and opposing handed player. The logical choice would be for the left handed person to win... The left handers were dangerous small percentage and so there style would never be the norm.'

Sawyer almost began thinking out loud "At least his ring crafted completely of sapphire was on the orthodox handed for an unmarried person - the left hand. "I thought you might need this" handing him the boomerang of Pinpin, when Styles saw it again he had a wave of *déjà vu*, then he became dizzy. His heart almost burst out his chest and he fell over, going silent.

He now found himself as a boy again among his people, the can-guru's and the Rock, the boomerang. It had all started with boomerang. He was awake outside the cave. Could it be a sign that he was on the right path? It had to be; there was no question about it. The dreaming knew more than he, as far as he could consequently remember and they had foretold the next seven years and he was to be involved in those events, whether his people lived or died in that time he would not know. That's what he took from it. He used the thought of things more than he did the actual using of the things, to his own amusement he thought.

Then as if nothing had happened he opened his eyes and was back on the floor of the deck of the ship. Standing up and without saying anything he put the boomerang in a sleeve of the red cape, so that it fit perfectly on his shoulders. Sawyer looked at him, bemused as to what he was doing. Stan said "You know, you can carry that thing in a place a lot better than that". He handed Sawyer a large Vessel issue backpack. As he took it by the sativa strap it cooed. "The blue dove" Stan said. "They picked it up back in Mauritius. It may save your life."

On deck they were met by the skivvy's of Stan, Theau and Leo, carried long spears of orchids. The purple and white petals beset the sweet fragrance of vanilla. The man called Loui, who had fallen from the mast shouted down on to the deck. "Weathers alright, no storms, high winds in a easterly direction". Back on deck Leo mumbled half smiling "Ici pour toi". Handing over the Orchid to Styles. Theau stood silent and took it all for a joke.

Sawyer inspected them. "Now tis rare these - Queen's of Madagascar. This should do fine". He walked to the starboard beam peering over the side of the Vessel. Styles followed him and looking down, he saw the reeded sailboat. Its silhouette refined and unchanged in thousands of years. The feeling he got from looking at the boat was like looking from the top of the world. The ancient waters of Lake Titicaca, like in the high lands miles from Machu Pichu.

The hand crafted vessel floated magnificently on top of the waters. Styles turned to Sawyer "Do you know". "Lets do this" Sawyer said cutting him off. He took a pocketknife and cut six inches from the stem of the orchid bulb. Placing it in his specially designed backpack. Stan gave Styles an empty string sack. He placed over his shoulder and was a handed a long spear orchid. He saw no need to cut the orchid. He simply made three hoops from the string bag then slid the orchid spear inside. Placing the sack on his shoulder he nodded to Theau who smiled back.

He hadn't realised, but Theau was a lot younger than his demeanour portrayed, he was the tallest and skinniest of the crew. The vibe he got from him was someone his own age. The world was a mad place and he wondered who had formed such a radical team of men with recruit's appearing wherever they were Vessel docked. Theau looked passed Styles and his smile turned to a horizontal line, neither smiling nor frowning. Lou shouted "Shes ready" Sawyer signalled to Lou so that he got the message. Turning to Theau he spat "Get the fuck out of here man, aint no time for smiles now, Focus on the mission,"

Leo slapped Theau on the arm. "Oniva! mec" then looked at Sawyer and said "Chow Styles". Suddenly the sky cracked. Styles didn't think it was too bizarre that Leo had not looked him in the eye. It seemed he was relaying a message more to Sawyer, than him. Hidden by the Vessel Sawyer and Styles climbed down the rope ladder to the reed boat. The design was warm to Styles reminding him of home. A place before he had come to Uluru. Two oars in hoop reeds extended both sides and were woven seamlessly.

Styles sat at the back, Sawyer at the front. From the Vessel there was a loud shout "HOWW!" it was Stan. Throwing down a thin cord, scraping Styles as it hit the ocean. With his eyes he followed the cord back on to the Vessel. Stan and Theau were on deck, hoisting a man sized bamboo kite up to Loui on the moon mast. The cord tightened and Sawyer had already attached it to the front of the reed boat. The wind had turned harsh and what felt no time at all.

The unfamiliar sky was a force to be reckoned with. The Vessel creaked as a large invisible force hid from their eyes. Sawyer attached a kite harness that had been set up on the reed boat bow. "Its going good" Loui shouted from the moon mast while lifting the kite in the air. Stan shouted to Sawyer to "Get ready". Sawyer put his bag down and told Styles to "get the oars ready". Styles picked up the oars. Sawyer content shouted, "Go". The cord shot up towards the kite. Sawyer stood up, taking the direction with his gloved hands. He looked at the sky and prayed to someone far off listening and watching. There were no stars to count on, no sun to ride with only the night and the wind. Stan shouted "Reet Man! Haweh YA GANNIN." He then looked up to see Loui release a secondary cord, Styles watched as the wingspan doubled in size.

As Loui let go, the wind lifted the kite high and fast

pushing it over the small boat. Styles looked up and saw the kite glowing faintly. "Sit down and hold on" Sawyer shouted. If Stan and Sawyer were this serious all the time maybe it was for good reason. Sitting back he did his best to hold on. Sawyer pulled on the cords, lessening the distance from boat to kite. The speed picked up 10 knots. The two cords straightened out and the full force of the kite could be felt. The front of the reed boat became raised out of the water. The kite worked perfectly, Styles had not had to row at all. Turning the two cords left and right Sawyer directed the boat out from the cover of the Vessel. Each time the boat hit a wave the speed picked up with the help of the winds.

Enduring the waves, they past the south coast of the Island guided by the Peruvian kite. The early morning winds blew the kite without rest. From the Vessel Stan was surely smiling, he thought. The device they had used to harness the wind lead them on to their goal. Looking back towards Vessel, lights illuminated a window under the back of the stern. Up and down the lights bounced as they rode wave after wave. "Head down". Surprised the kite crash in to the waters beside them. It stretched as long as the boat. Sawyer screamed, "ROW". Styles clutched them and began to row frantically. Sawyer searched for his knife to cut the cord from the harness. Once again screaming to someone far off and omnipresent. Sawyer must have been navigating by smell.

"Where are we going?" Styles screamed. There was no answer from the captain. Styles looked back, all he could see was the night. It was the same when he looked forward. "Can you not feel it?". Sawyer shouted. "Styles was confused and stopped rowing for only a second "Do not stop rowing, a good sailor knows where he is coming from and where he is going. Just keep rowing."

Styles just focused on his rhythm. Then Styles realised that since Sawyer had not looked in the direction of the

Island of Sante Marie for some time he must have a way to navigate. He had only focused on going forward. The clouds and wind had left them. He looked up to see the stars were now out. "By my reckoning we shall soon be coming up to Madagascar, here I will take over roving."

Sawyer rowed onward. As the journey continued he wondered how different Sante Marie would be to Madagascar. Styles could hear the bird cooing from inside thee bag cage. Stroke after stroke - sweat wiped from the face with shoulder bones. Splash after splash, wave after wave. Keep going, he thought to himself, Sawyer didn't even blink, the man was hell bent on his arrival. An hour later Sawyers arms were dead and the sea was calm and cold.

"We are about half way, if we continue at this speed we should be there in one hour." Styles had no need to stop and enjoy the break; he took over the rowing once more. As he did, he zoned out of thinking of anything but the pain in his arms. The sky was beginning to show light in the west. He knew he'd learnt in those few months travelling with the Southern Cross to use the sky as a guide across ocean. Like the never changing diamonds in the night sky, the liberties he had on the Vessel were unique.

He thought about the place they were going to and realised the only thing he knew was what not to expect. He did not expect to be greeted with fellow brother and sister's who were separated only by intelligence. The smart or educated could travel freely throughout the world, being left to their own devices and means. As ideological as it was to believe the world was like, he now knew he could not expect this greeting. For if these humans on the Vessel could travel so strategically, who could be safe from their targets. The bitter answer was no one. Absolutely no one. The truth was a little difficult to swallow coupled with the fact he was the sole person to help his people out of any slump they had found themselves in. He spewed a little in his mouth and spat it out in to the ocean. The sickening feeling that the rest of the people across the planes, as kind as they thought themselves to be, they were screwed unless they were to help their fellow man.

On he rowed, the strength of his determination doubled, his paced and he found he had to stop thinking about his peoples plight, or at least relax a little. Sawyer's speed was fast enough; he would waste his own energy going any faster. If only the distance was smaller. Unfortunately it wasn't. The sun had not miraculously reappeared and the moon was far from view, wherever it was. He was fading in and out of memory with all the exertion. All he knew was to row. Row, after row. It was quite ridiculous when he thought about it and he laughed out loud.

He kept rowing but he couldn't hold up his head. Darkness all around him, apart from one faint speckle on the floor, He was unsure where the speck of light had come from, but there it was. Then he realised he was looking at his own hand; it was the sapphire ring on his finger. Through all the friction of rowing the ring once again glowed with tribo-luminescence. How ridiculous he thought that of all the light in the entire ocean. All he could see was coming from his left hand, not Sawyer or the Vessel or any of those humans.

On he kept rowing, knowing he had to keep going. Once he was there he could rest. Arms that swelled and sweated. Until then he would have to press on. He had questions to ask about where they were going but it never seemed the right time. Drawing breath of life took up the moments between rows. He was no longer smiling or laughing for that matter. He was core bent on getting the fuck off the boat and on to the problems that would arise.

He decided to go deeper into thought and concentrate on nothing, until the point where the only thing he would see was the shore. He would just zone out and ignore anything but rowing and the repetitive rhythm, using it like a heartbeat. No more erratic movements or thinking. Controlling his breathing and pushing on, he soon found the crazy fear that had encroached on him had left, replaced by the calm cool knowing that he was on a boat in the dark going to a specified destination. After that thought, he managed to flip back into the nothingness.

Every sixteen strokes he looked up at the sky to make sure he was on the correct trajectory. On and on they went in unison, untethered by the lack of weather. From what he gathered, looking upon the stars they were on correct trajectories. He had no way of knowing how fast or for how long they had travelled for, they were the deciding factors in knowing just how far along they had came along.

Without realising he just blurted out. "Why are we really coming to this Island, tell me or Ill tip this fucking boat right now". Sawyer surprised by the mysterious question out of nowhere. "The last thing I heard from you was laughing, and that had been a good hour ago. What's all this about?". That's his response, he thought to himself. Although it wasn't the answer he wanted he thought about it. Obviously Sawyer had to be careful what information to hand out, even if it was just the two of them in middle of the ocean.

Still in a moment of fury, brought on by their unusual situation and with no one but the two of them to do anything. Styles stopped rowing and raised the oar in to the boat. Sawyer thought about reaching for his knife that was tucked in to his ankle. Then he thought against it. He was somewhat brain boggled and in a conundrum. On one hand he needed to get to Madagascar with Styles in tow, but he didn't appreciate the ultimatum he had been placed in.

He was unsure whether to teach Styles or choke the life out of him. He resisted the urge. That fateful urge to spin around and knock the man from his seated position and in to the ocean below leaving him to drowned. If he had any brains Styles he would be on guard right now. Styles could feel the tension rising on the boat as the silence continued. The wind howled "Tell me something at least", giving Sawyer a way out of the madness. Sawyer thought long and hard. "Okay we are to go to see the King of Madagascar, there is long celebration where we might meet him. I seek an audience with him."

Styles had got something from him he had not expected. The truth. The darkness had been all around for sometime now. Out of nowhere the pigeon spoke, as if waking from a sleep. The beak buzzed from the agitated ether between them. On and on, his beak throbbed. Sawyer became like the bird he thought to himself. If he could talk, he wouldn't. Instead he might cry a little or acquire a lump in the back of his throat. Still Styles was beyond words. Only feelings.

He began to row again. He saw irony of the situation. Here he was on a boat with a man who he was quite sure was about to kill him had it not been for the fact he was needed. Travelling in the dead of night across deadly waters and yet the amazing feeling that came was from the comical animal. All could see the pigeon's end game. To be free from the cage, even if it did not look like one. Thinking of anything else was near impossible, for the pigeon. He had been in high thought for so long that all he could remember was the depths of despair the pigeon spoke. He remembered to say none of this out loud.

Suddenly he could see a shore. Sunlight. He could feel it now. The light blue light mellowed. Pointing towards him, he felt it, just like the pigeon could and the human in front of him. But he hoped he did. He counted on the sun to guide the way for all. It had been quite good at doing that. The light was the promise he hoped to counteract the hardship that had fell upon his life that night - something as reassuring as the morning light. The air was warmer now, upon his legs, his right cheek. He glared in to the sunlight full on, remembered like the rotation of the sun and moon. Forever he would again embrace the light of morning. His record would soon again be up to scratch. For if he ever did meet his people again. He cut himself short of that thought. Solar gazing in itself provided enough substance for this lifetime. That was enough he told himself, he did not need more.

A fish jumped in to the boat as if on cue. To his right and moving towards to the light the ocean gave up a myriad of sea creatures. Fish upon fish jumped out of the calm. Behind the boat, what sounded like a wave collapsing and soon after the wave was felt. Styles turned his neck to see as a whale. Clear out of the water, glistening gold's in the morning light. The tail of another dropped below the bubbling awakening waters. Sawyer shouted something but it was impossible to focus.

Looking towards him the light illuminating his beardy face. Strange it was, behind Sawyer all was dark, black almost. Was it night time in front of him and light behind him? All he saw was two large blue moons in darkness behind Sawyer. He lifted his eyes to see if the sky was still there, it was. The black wall was in fact a whale and not the one he had seen. The wall was coming down 20 feet from them. The two crescent moons hitting the ocean like the eyes of a whale. If the awe had finished there, he may still have held his oar, but the black wall was still coming down. Towering in front of them like Uluru.

"TURN!!" Sawyer shouted. Styles looked at Saywer, he could have sworn when he caught his gaze that he was not looking at Sawyer but the pale tormented Hagar of a man who was had recently returned from death. His face chimneyed a slow cold steam and his eyes were darker then they had ever been. In this moment he saw Sawyer, as he would be on his final day. If it were not that day, that face would again return. He knew he had woken something but was not sure what.

Sawyer, using his paddle frantically sploshed the starboard side. Styles looked down spotting the fish that puffed at him in the blink of an eye. Not yet he thought to himself, infuriated with the machine of death they were in. At least that's what the inhabitant of the water's said to him. Grabbing the other oar he hit the water with the speed strength and rhythm of an able bodied sailor. In and out in and out, he had become accustomed to the sea lie easier than he could have imagined.

As the tower became a house, the view returned and the tail of the great whale came down in its final motif. It was obvious they were getting a big slap. Again he could feel time slowing down. Maybe the same was happening for Sawyer or anyone that might find themselves in a dangerous situation, where they might have only a second or two to do something or feel unruly wrath. So it was without anymore thought that he jumped out of the boat throwing first the paddle. As the tail of the whale came down on them there was not much they could to stop it. The autochthon had not stopped to contemplate his action.

As he dived out of the boat with as much effort as the small fish had taken to get in to the boat he found himself merely scraping across the port side - if it ever had one. His ankle was strapped in to something still on the boat. In this moment he realised if he was surely to die then ankle would be lost and he would never be able to save his friends family mother, and countless brothers and sister's. Who all eagerly awaited him solely to complete his mission that hade fallen so naturally on him. For his people could not dream the future anymore that he could dive in to the great deep.

The look of Tjikurpa upon them was the exquisite measure of their souls. There was nothing but admiration for the life they had known. Sawyer looked up at the Shadow. 'Come on ya bastard' he shouted. Styles merely managed a square look in the direction of the cove. And then it was done. The tail hit the entire boat, all at the same time. The front, the back, the side and the top.

The shadow became smooth skin. The entire boat under its wing, sucking all light away replacing it with water darkness an pain. At some point the technology of the boat took effect. Sawyer had been flung out of the cocoon, sucked by the departing wailing tail. Yet he swam under immense pressure to get back to the boat. Styles unable to anything but to flail about under the current he found himself in.

Sawyer raced to get back to what was his life – fighting to stay away from what was not. On he screamed until the cold waters were satisfied. The boat proceeded to float again, the water drained out from the sides. Up and up it went. Unsure of anything other than to trust in Hawah, he screamed words of joy, choking on his shortness of breath, he stopped short, instead focussing on his well-being. Sawyer reached the side of the boat. Styles was so disoriented he could not do anything but breathe for life. Sawyer climbed aboard. More waves found there way to them, however were no match for the wall. In to the distance were more whales and further away, still on the horizon, the majesty of Madagascar - only a mile or so away.

The two paddled with their arms until Sawyer clutched an oar from the abyss. The boat dipped again, though he did not care. He needed it, he wanted it, and he would die for it. "Fuckin Yah" he shouted as he jumped back in to the dark waters, seeing something Styles could not. A couple of minutes later Sawyer returned one again to the boat with the second oar in the shape of a long thick tree branch, thick enough to be used as an oar. "We cant be far away, either that fuckin whale picks his gums with this stick or land is not that far. Either way its a blessing, now row motherfucker row". Soon the movement of the waves could not hurt them.

Realising something, Sawyer jumped up with a fright.

Frantically turning, he opened the bag to see the situation of the bird. Unsure if it was dead he poked it and Styles blew at it. The bird began to move about eventually fluttering its wings. Sawyer looked at Styles as if nothing had happened that day, trying to hide the solemn look, as if remembering the arrival of the whales. But Styles knew, he had seen the fear.

Closing the bird back in the backpack. Sawyer took the thick barky branch and began to row. On they pushed towards Madagascar. As they neared the shore Sawyer said to Styles. "What do you know of Madagastar, known as Enkidu, its body is here for all to see".

Styles had no idea what he was talking about. Still Styles listened. "The giant of stone that cut down the great forest of the earth." Styles eyes brightened. Parched for words he said. "The chiant that cut the tree down". Sawyer smiled, "yes it is here, I know it. They say a bishop came across it once and named it s such, but they are just words. Almeida doesn't care about such things. He seeks only his family legacy and the information the king here can give him. You seek to change the world, I can see it, only together can we all achieve our goals, in this life or the next".

They could smell the rocky shore and felt the warm breeze.

GLOSSARY

straliyah - Australia

Uluru – Ayres Rock, a giant pebble shaped rock that is approx. 6 miles in circumference

PinPin, Also CanFather – Styles's father

Can-Garoo - Kangaroo

Kalkatungan – Style's tribe

Tjikurpa- the dream world, where people communicate , also the universe, also the real world

Jah Vah – the area that Style's tribe live in.

Greater Vandea - One of the 3 Vandea's

Printed in Poland
by Amazon Fulfillment
Poland Sp. z o.o., Wrocław

54600286R00108